PERSONAL PAN

A COMFORT FOOD ROMANCE

DARLENE EVERLY

DARLENE EVERLY

Personal Pan

A COMFORT FOOD ROMANCE

WA, USA

Personal Pan is just the beginning of the Comfort Food romances, if you would like to be the first to hear about the next book in the series, get a free book, as well as see what else the author has written, please go to darleneeverly.com and sign up for her newsletter.

Happily Ever Cooking!

To request use of the copyrighted material, please contact the author at darleneeverly.com
Hardcover: ISBN 978-1-954719-08-8
Paperback: ISBN 978-1-954719-07-1
Ebook: ISBN 978-1-954719-06-4
First paperback edition February 2021.
Edited by Beth Hale, Magnolia Editing.
Cover art by Jupiter Alley.
Layout by Beth Hale, Magnolia Editing.

WA, US

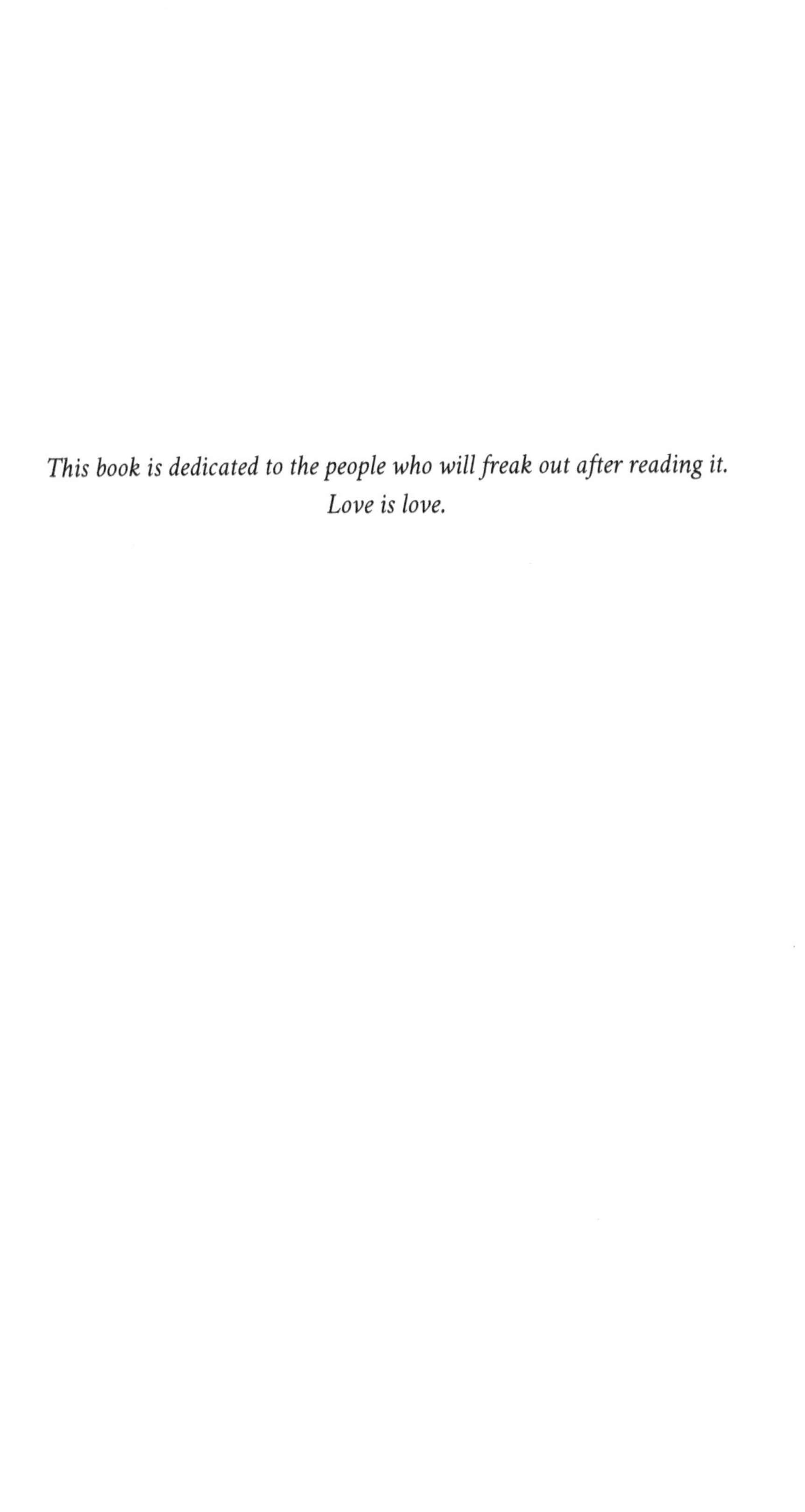

This book is dedicated to the people who will freak out after reading it.
Love is love.

CHAPTER 1

*E*veryone loves the smell of pizza except me. It stopped being exciting at age eight, when a girl in my class invited everyone but me to her birthday party, which she held in my dad's pizza restaurant. Watching your classmates have fun when you've been deliberately left out of tends to tarnish all the things you associate with the memory. For me, that's pizza.

Now, I'm freshly minted eighteen, and I'm starting to hate the smell. I still like the taste, but one too many times I've walked into school and someone has sniffed the air like a dog and wondered aloud if there was pizza for lunch later.

And then there's right now. Friday night after a football game, we're open until two for the beer money, and I'm behind the counter entering a bill into the register. Cash, with $1.25 tip left for me.

Gee, thanks.

At least this bill is from someone I don't know. Not that it matters. The people I do know from school pretend they've never seen me before when I have an apron on and an order pad in my hand. Which, come to think of it, isn't that different than at school. Maybe they honestly don't know who I am beyond a vague recollection of their lab partner who smelled of garlic bread sticks, Dad's famous sauce, and pepperoni.

I wipe down the table the couple who paid just vacated, knowing if I don't someone will be horrified by the crumbs inside of five minutes. Sure enough, the gust of fall chill I feel as I stretch to get the furthest corner of the table announces the arrival of more customers.

"Hey, Olivia. I was hoping you would be here tonight," Theresa Moreland says from behind me and I feel my face heat in response.

My brain short circuits and I miss the opportunity to make a joke out of the sad fact that I'm here every night. Instead, I stand up slowly to turn and face her, trying desperately to get my cheeks to shut up and stop yelling to the universe that not too long ago I was crazy about this girl.

"Hi, Theresa," I say, glancing up to meet her eyes for only a moment and staring back at the rag in my hand and the black and white tile floor.

"Yeah. Um, listen, I know you said we're fine, but I just want to make sure, because I really like you—as a friend." She's quick to correct and it hurts a little more. "And I want us to stay friends."

This is worse than being at the birthday party I wasn't invited to. This is the most awkward thing, in a series of painfully awkward things, to ever happen to me at work. My eyes are looking anywhere but her face, trying to decide if the whole world knows what's happening in this corner, on this Friday. I'm getting dumped, again.

"Yeah," I say. "No problem."

She pulls me in for a tentative and careful hug, and I have to think about how many more pounds of flour I need to include in the next order to accommodate the season change and the increase in customers that comes with it. I have to focus on the intricacies of the calculations formed of equal parts knowledge of previous business and instinct, that I almost do automatically, to keep from crying.

She lets go of me and wanders to one of the noisier tables in the middle of the restaurant. The same one her cheerleading squad always occupies because they can squeeze more people around it than the alcoves or the booths.

I sniff back more tears and put my fake it until you make it face on. These football players and cheerleaders always talk a big game about putting everything out of their minds to perform. They know nothing.

Every day I have to pretend I'm a shiny, happy person and the customer is always right. Even if I'm in abject misery and the customer is an utter jackass.

But Theresa isn't a jackass. She's just not into me. She thought she was for a while, and I get that. I'm challenging, and she... doesn't want me.

I swallow hard, and go back to the bussing station to drop off the rag and dishes of the table I'd just cleared. Maybe it would be easier to pretend I'm great, that my smile is genuine, if my work took any cognitive labor at all. It doesn't. While I take orders, greet guests, get drinks, and order the cooks around, I stew in my mind.

My last three relationships haven't just failed; they've left me an increasingly messed up wreck.

There's the non-binary person from the next district over who I dated for three months before they realized they were into guys—while we were making out. Which, not their fault, and not mine. I'm glad they figured themselves out, and I can't offer them what they want, so that's cool. But damned if the timing didn't suck completely. It took me a while after that to get the nerve to even try again.

The guy who I did finally decide to try again with I still see all the time. My dad's best friend's son. I'm still not convinced the entire relationship wasn't more about our parents pushing us together than it was about what either of us really wanted. It didn't last long. Two months. In large part because it was like trying to kiss a wet sock. Before we got together, I liked him, he liked me. We flirted, a lot, and our parents pushed so we tried. From the first moment our lips touched, we both knew it was over. We had a ton of chemistry until we had zero.

Theresa was my last relationship, which was never really a relationship. We never went public. She was always afraid to. Although I doubt anyone in our lives would care; this is Seattle. But I didn't want to push her into outing herself before she was ready, so we kept it quiet. To anyone really paying attention, I'm sure we were a lot less quiet than we thought. My mom knew, my dad knew, my brother even looked at me weird when he came home from school one weekend and we were there. But in the whole of the eight months we dated, my parents never questioned. They just accepted that yes, I had dates, one was with a guy, and now I have a girlfriend. Had.

My mom complemented me on my taste, because according to her it didn't matter the gender, her daughter always found beautiful, kind people.

Well, one of those beautiful, kind people is sitting at her usual table and she keeps glancing under her eyelashes at Rebecca, another cheerleader.

Oh.

That sucks.

I gulp down a breath filled to bursting with the laughter of other people and try again to focus on my immediate surroundings and forget the ache in my chest.

Then, there he is. Omar Martinez. The perfect distraction in the form of the perfect boy. He smiles his blinding, beautiful smile and waves to me as he walks in the door.

He never fails to look for me and acknowledge my presence before taking his seat. Tonight, though, he adds a level of knee quaking, heart gone berserk, dear god what am I going to do to his entrance, by bee lining right for me.

"Hey, Olivia. Busy in here tonight," Omar says, leaning against the counter while I forget how to count the tip left over from the bill I'm entering and have to ignore him for a second to try again.

"Hey, Omar. Yeah, always busy on Fridays. I'm surprised you weren't here earlier; the team already left," I say, trying not to let him know how difficult it is for me to talk to him. He was part of the problem in my relationship with Theresa. We both think he's perfect, but she never fully believed that doesn't mean I want to date him. I mean, if he asked me now, yes. But when I was committed to her? No way. I'm perfectly happy to keep enjoying him from this comfortable, not too worried about making a fool of myself distance.

"I'll catch up to them later, I brought someone I want you to meet. My cousin, Campbell," Omar says, and gestures behind him to where a slightly taller, much reedier, and less angular version of Omar stands.

"Hi," Campbell says and my brain stutters. The voice is musical and soft, not a voice I can qualify in my meager categories. "He, him," he says, and my face is immediately on fire with a blush.

Wait, did he say? Oh. Okay.

Before I can make an even bigger ass of myself, or before my blush betrays me anymore, I shove my hand forward to shake his.

"Hi, nice to meet you. I'm Olivia, she, her," I say. His shake is firm, his hands graceful and long fingered like a pianist's. He reminds me of an anime character made flesh.

"Campbell just moved here and is living with us now. He's being homeschooled, but he's a senior like us. I was thinking that you're about the coolest person I know, so he should meet you first," Omar says, rushing through his words, which he never does. He usually has the ease of a cat, but there's something off about him right now.

"That's nice; thanks, Omar. Wait…" I say and smile because I think I know what he really means, but I'll gladly soak up the compliments.

"Are you just introducing us because you want to get Campbell a job?" I ask.

"No! I mean, yeah, that would be awesome, but that isn't why." Omar talks over himself in the rush to get the words out and Campbell laughs.

"He really did say you were cool and that we should meet. He thinks I need friends and he said you would be a good one," Campbell says and pushes Omar with his elbow a bit.

"Okay, Campbell. Well, as my new friend, you should know I am exceedingly boring and spend almost all my time at school or at work," I say, with a gesture to encompass the restaurant.

"I spend almost all my time at home, so actually your life sounds really exciting," Campbell says, with an air about him that makes me relax.

"If you're serious about a job, we could use someone in the kitchen; we need help washing dishes and keeping up with the prep," I say. And we do, it isn't a lie, but we've needed that for more than a month, and this is the first thing I've done about it.

Maybe I just need more of Campbell's calming influence, maybe I just want to prove to Omar how cool I really am. I don't know, but we could use the help, and this is as good a shot as I've had to have a real say in who gets hired, so I'm skirting my dad and taking it. He won't notice with all that's been going on.

"That's great, thanks, Olivia," Campbell says, beaming.

"I told you she was the best," Omar says.

And my Friday night is magically much, much better.

CHAPTER 2

fter I close up for the night, I head upstairs to our house. Well, our apartment, but since it's the only other thing inside the restaurant building, I always call it a house. It was, once upon a time, a cool turn of the century grand dame on Capital Hill. Now, it's still that but it's been converted to suit our family's needs. Which means that while I love this house, the creaky old hardwood floors, and my absolutely to die for turret of a bedroom, the restaurant smells always waft through the old girl and our house never smells like anything other than food.

Tiptoeing through my darkened home, I stop by my parent's room first. It's on the other side of the house from mine, but if Mom is having a bad night, I need to coordinate opening with Dad so he can get some sleep.

Their door is ajar and the blue light from the TV washes the room in an inconsistent glow making the collection of pill bottles, creams, and a million cups and discarded tissue on my mother's nightstand look less intrusive than they actually are.

Cancer has broken into our house and threatened my moth-

8

er's life. It's a villain with zero redeeming qualities and the only tragic past is in the lives it's already taken.

I take a deep breath and bury the anger at this disease that has taken us all hostage.

Mom and Dad are both sleeping, so I slowly pull their door closed and head to my room. I have to do payroll before I go to sleep and, hopefully, I'll still be awake enough to get some homework done.

In my room, settled at my desk with the timecards in front of me I realize my damn brother has done it again. There's a timecard for the last two weeks with his name at the top and eighty hours written in, eighty hours he did *not* work. And there, at the bottom, is my dad's signature.

Damn it, Dad. What the hell?

My dad and I have had this discussion, over and over again. With mom's medical bills, and still paying on the loans we took out so we could pay our whole staff during the lockdown, we cannot afford to be paying my brother for work he doesn't do. This isn't going to be his business one day; it's going to be mine. It makes me crazy that my dad doesn't let me run it how it needs to be run.

I'm sure Dad wanted Joey Junior to take over running Joe's when he started the restaurant a year after my brother was born, but Junior is becoming a doctor, and Dad will never admit out loud that he wishes it were any different than it's turned out.

My brother is a brat. A spoiled rotten brat. And I'm tired of him stealing from my business. It would be different if he worked here at all, but he only shows up during breaks for the tip money and the chance to hit on girls. He only calls once a week to check on Mom. He's not the one who has to help her. He's not the one who has to watch the chemo break down her body while it supposedly kills the cancer. He's going to be a damn doctor, and he's right at the University of Washington, a quick bus ride away, but does he come to check on the most important patient I can think of? No. Good old Junior just keeps shining in his golden glow while leaving little Olivia to build his halos.

I drop my face into my hands and rub my temples. It pisses me off so bad there's a sour taste in my mouth.

No. Not this time. Junior can go to Dad all he wants. I've been running most of the business for months, and for months before Mom got sick, I was doing a lot. So, I'm going to be the boss I am. He doesn't get to treat my business like his own personal college fund anymore. He's most of the way done with school anyway, he can actually work for what he wants to get paid, or he can take out some student loans. That's not on me, or the business, or Dad trying to juggle Mom's care and the money at the same time anymore. That's on Junior.

Dad is just going to have to come to me and talk about it if he wants to keep doing this, he can't sign this stupid time card like a coward.

I tear the time card to shreds and put it in my trash can.

Maybe I have enough energy for homework after all, because that felt good.

CHAPTER 3

It's Campbell's first day on the job; seven A.M. to prep dough, and deserts, and the chopping for the lunch crowd that always comes in a steady stream on Saturdays from our ten A.M. open until we close at two A.M. Dad calls all Saturday the lunch rush, because it starts and it never ends.

Campbell is in for one hell of a trial by wood fired pizza. I snort a laugh to myself and he looks up at me with a hurt look while he struggles to tie his apron in the back.

"Sorry, I was laughing at a dumb pun I just thought of. Can I help you with that?" I ask and shake my head at my own ability to be a complete doofus.

He raises one brow at me, in that universal you might be crazy look, but he drops the ties of his apron and turns around offering his back by way of answer.

"Here's the trick, you wrap the ties around to your front," I say, taking his ties and turning him, wrapping him in the process, then I tie his apron strings in the front. When I look up, I'm incredibly close to him. His skin is flawless and this close to him I realize there are green flecks in his brown eyes, and he doesn't smell like pizza. He smells like rain from his walk into the restaurant, and peaches.

"Why do you smell like peaches?" I blurt out before my brain can filter my stupid, impulsive mouth.

He chuckles and says, "That's my shampoo." Still smirking he continues, "Not all guys use crap products."

"Oh." I give a small laugh and step back to try and cover for my uncouth words. "I guess just my dad and brother, huh?"

"Speaking of your dad, he's my boss, right? When will I meet the famous Joe?" he asks, going to the sink to wash his hands.

I roll my eyes and I no longer feel bad for unintentionally insulting him about his products.

"My dad is with my Mother today; she has appointments," I say, reciting the usual excuse so I don't have to talk about my mother's cancer, waiting for him to finish washing up while I plant my hands on my hips. It's best we get this over with right away anyway before he makes an ass of himself. Although maybe I should let him.

"And I'm your boss. Who do you think is the manager here?" I'm so tired of people assuming I have no power; this is my restaurant.

"Oh, I'm sorry. It's just his name on the sign, and you're still in high school." He has the grace to look genuine in his chagrin.

"I'm the one who does payroll, and when my dad retires, this place is mine. That makes me the boss." Don't be more stupid right now, please. I don't want to fire Omar's cousin, that wouldn't win me any points with Omar.

"Cool," he says, and offers me a wide smile. "A girl boss. I like it. Okay, boss, what now?"

His immediate acceptance, even a small level of celebration, makes me pull my hands off my hips and think maybe I misjudged his question, maybe it really was just the name on the sign.

Good.

"First, the dough; you just have to follow the instructions printed right there," I say, "and I'll start the sauce. When we get done, we'll start the chop, but that will be what you spend most of the day doing, the chop. I only allow so much at a time." The whole time I'm talking I'm walking through the kitchen gathering the things we'll need.

"I don't really know what any of what you said means, but I'll just follow the instructions," he says, wandering after me through the kitchen.

"Let me get this sauce started and I'll walk you through the first of your dough."

"The first of my dough? Out of context, that sounds like you're a mobster giving me a bribe, or a threat," he says, and shrugs his shoulders.

I can't help it, I smile. That is something I never thought I would be compared to, a mobster.

"Maybe I should get a zoot suit, or look up a Bonnie costume," I say, starting on my tasks.

He smiles back at me and follows my lead, doing what I do, or simply anticipating what I'm reaching for and getting to it first.

"I think hiring you was a very good decision," I say, the third time he hands me something before I can reach for it.

"You're only saying that to butter my biscuits, so I'll set you up with my cousin," he says back, staring down at the garlic he's mincing.

"Uh…" Well, I'm not, but I can't say it didn't cross my mind when I did hire him. And how the hell does he know I'm into Omar?

"It's cool. I know, he's everything and all the girls love him. It's part of the reason I'm living at his place this year," he says.

My hands still in the dough I'm kneading. His voice holds

some sadness, some indefinable ache that makes me sore in response. I don't think I'm going to like his answer to the question I know I have to ask. No one opens up their pain like that, unless they want to talk about it.

"What do you mean?" I ask, my voice hushed.

"It was the bargain I struck with my mother in the Dominican Republic, where I'm from. My dad was from the states, but I've lived with my mom in the DR my whole life and don't talk to my dad much. She said if I wanted to learn to be a man I had to live with my cousin."

"What the hell? That doesn't make sense. There are as many ways to be a man as there are men," I say, punching the dough for emphasis. I'm so mad my eyes are welling with tears. I hate angry crying, which just makes it harder to stop them.

"She is supportive and loves me. She's trying her best," he says, taking a deep breath and looking up at me. His mouth drops open and he backs away from the counter with his hands up and his eyes wide.

"I'm not crying... This is what happens when I get mad... Stop looking at me like that... It will make it worse," I say, taking deep breaths between my sentences, gulping down air to try and stop the stupid traitorous tears I wipe away with my forearm because I have flour all over my hands.

"Damn, seriously, I'm sorry." He's fumbling over his words, not completing his sentences and grabs some napkins, shoving them at me, arms outstretched.

"Just stop... talking. You being nice... makes it worse," I say, using the napkins in a frantic pawing at my own face to stem the tide of tears. "Gahhhh!" I sniff, and finally I'm done. My tears come to a stop and all I'm left with are blobs of soaked napkins stuck to my face along with bits of flour.

"I'm," I start, and take a deep breath while a smile creeps across his face, "going to clean up."

I try to ignore the stifled laughter that follows me to the employee bathroom. Of course, this would happen. Of course, it would happen in front of Campbell so now he'll go tell Omar how much of a mess I am.

The water is cool on my overheated face as I rinse all the evidence from my skin and out of my hairline, checking in the mirror it's all gone, and the whole while steeling myself for having to face Campbell again after being so embarrassed.

Yep, this is exactly what will help me get Omar to date me so I can get over Theresa, perfect plan. Make a complete ass of myself and win his, what, sympathy date? Ugh.

Walking back into the kitchen, I try and keep from looking too closely at Campbell. But after a half hour of working, feeling his eyes on me the whole time because they have to be to follow what I'm doing so he can learn what he needs to do, I know. This can't continue.

Turning to face him full on and looking him in the eye, I suck down a quick breath that tastes like fear and adrenaline. I really don't want to have this conversation, but here goes nothing. "I'm sorry I freaked you out by crying. It's not something I have much control over when I get screaming, murderously angry."

"Really, I was more worried about you than freaked, and..." He trails off and stares at me, his hand reaches out toward me only to fall back to his side without touching me, or doing whatever it was he was planning on doing. He drops his head and draws in a deep breath before looking at me again.

"I appreciate that you were so concerned for me, your first reaction was righteous anger on my behalf," he says.

"Righteous? Nah, just decent. Hey, I, uh..." Crap, how do I ask this? "Look, I just got dumped by my girlfriend," I say, bumbling my way through my words.

"Oh," is all he says. Just a surprised chirp of sound and then nothing.

"I mean, I've dated other people, including a guy, and an enby, I'm just into who I'm into, but that isn't the point." I drag a breath in and will myself to stop rambling. "It's just that, I was hoping, I mean." This is *not* going well. Just spit it out, brain. "Okay, so I have always liked your cousin, and I was hoping that he liked me too and that maybe he would want to go out with me. So, I was really, really hoping you would maybe not tell Omar about how much of a mess I am?"

This is almost worse than the disaster I made of myself. I can't believe I just admitted all of that. Oh, god, I'm pathetic. I look down at the floor instead of at him, not wanting to see his reaction when it crosses his face, just preferring for this moment to look at my own feet.

He puts both his hands on my shoulders and my head pops up to look at him, this is not what I was expecting. He's grinning. A smile full of knowing and glee is getting bigger by the second and taking over his face.

I'm not so sure this is great for me.

"I didn't know you were this cute when you were into someone," he says, all grin with his head cocked to the side so I don't have to tilt my head back as far to look into his eyes as I normally do.

"You're not... mad?"

"That you hired me to get a good in with my cousin? No. But tell me about this girlfriend, because Omar thinks you're straight," he says and steps away from me, going back to prepping.

"Well, she wasn't ready for people to know. But, wait. How do you know he thinks I'm straight?" I go back to my work alongside him, more comfortable than I've been in a while.

"When he suggested I get a job with his friend, I asked. For some reason being trans means half the straight people I know only want to introduce me to other queers. He explained that you're straight but cool. He has no idea," he says, mincing garlic.

"Oh. Okay," I say, getting back into the groove of dough making.

"So, he thinks you haven't gone out with anyone for a while, right?"

"Well, yeah. So?"

"Do you think he knows you're into him?" he asks.

"No. I mean, not until recently did I really think about it. Before that I was with someone and Omar was just someone decent who was fun to look at. When she broke up with me I was torn up about it for a while, but he's always so nice so it was easy to imagine a rebound with him as the soft landing I guess," I say, kneading the dough in rhythm so that my voice takes on the same cadence as the movements of my body.

"Wow, that's so romantic," he says, sarcasm dripping from his voice.

"Hey, I didn't say I was romantic, just, you know, looking," I say. And he raspberries out a breath. He actually raspberries at me. "What the hell?"

"I'm sorry," he says, and smiles to soften the blow. "Did you have a thing for him before you dated your girlfriend?"

"Yes, actually. Not a thing really, but I thought he was pretty perfect, good looking, fun, gets good grades, and is genuinely nice to everyone,"

"Well, he is, but…" Campbell trails off and I peek up at him, expecting some big dark secret, instead I see he's smiling one half of his mouth and squinting at me.

"What?"

"I think we need to do something drastic."

CHAPTER 4

"Drastic?" I squint at Campbell. Nope. It doesn't matter how closely I look; I can't figure out where he's going with that. "I'm not sure I want to know what you mean."

"I think he might be into you, but he doesn't realize you even want to date. Anyone. At all," he says and bites his lip.

Whatever the next thing out of his mouth is going to be I don't think I'll like it, what he just said is gutting as is. "I know… I'm not very social, but mostly I'm just busy," I say, trying to put a light spin on what I know is a problem, my lack of real connection to anyone but this place and my family.

"I get that. You're a boss, literally. You do a lot, and it doesn't leave a lot of time, but that's why I think we need to come up with a plan to let him know you want to do things," he says, and I laugh until I snort.

"Oh, god. You heard that?" I say while he tries, and fails, to stifle a laugh. "You said, *things*. It was very heavy innuendo." Which only makes him laugh harder.

"No, you know what I mean. And the snort was cute," he says.

My face heats in a blush that could not be timed worse. My stupid face. It always does this. Who needs to worry about choosing their words carefully when half the time your own face betrays whatever ridiculous thing passes through your head? I take a breath and try to focus back on the ominous drastic measures he thinks I need to employ in my social life.

"But I don't know what you think I can do, short of walking up to Omar and asking him out, which I am way too freaked out about talking to people in general to ever do that," I say, with a punch into a new pile of dough I imagine as my own personality failings.

"I think there's a way we can let him know you like dating without you putting yourself in a position that would freak you out. He already thinks you're great, and he's seen you so we know he knows you're adorable, now he just needs to know you're willing," he says, taking some of my already prepped crusts to the walk in, leaving me to think about what he's said for a minute.

I'm adorable? That's a new one. I would say painfully average. Brown hair, brown eyes, small and short. I suppose I have nice lips; would I date me? Hmm…

"Hey, what if," he yells from the walk in, pausing until he gets back to help me again. When he gets to me, one half of his mouth is in that puckish smile again, it makes me stand up straighter and gulp. "What if we go on a fake date to show him you're up for the idea."

"Campbell! Be serious,' I say, laughing. "That would never work."

"It would. It would cement your coolness to him, going on a few pity dates with me, and it would simultaneously prove you're up for dates at all and that he's into you because his jealousy would pop up," he says, and leans toward me across the island.

My heart does some dance moves in my chest, his plan makes me nervous.

"You don't need anyone's pity date, Campbell." My face is on fire. "You know that. And there's no way any of this idea works out the way you think," I say, and keep back the fact that I think this could blow up like a grease fire, the kind you can't put out with water, but need to smother. In this scenario I'm pretty sure I would be the one to end up smothered in an inability to ever put myself out there to date again.

His face gets all melty and soft, and I want to hide, until I realize what he's doing, "Wait, you're practicing! Stop looking at me like that."

He straightens up and laughs, shaking his head. Hopefully it will clear the crazy ideas from his brain. I stretch my back and refocus on my work, this whole conversation is bananas.

"Just think about it, if you decide you need my help…" he says, passing me another block of cheese to shred.

My cheeks flame again and my back tenses up. I get the feeling I'm going to be thinking about it a lot.

We're almost ready to open, all the prep is done, and the sound of my dad's heavy footsteps on the stairs that connect the restaurant to our house announces his arrival before his deep voice calls out a, "Hello."

"Hey, Dad. This is Campbell, I hired him yesterday," I say, gesturing to where Campbell is restocking the straws at the bussing station.

"Hi Campbell, glad you're here," my dad says, and Campbell shakes his outstretched hand. My dad looks back at me and raises his eyebrows.

"Olivia, I need to talk to you quickly before we open," he says, as Nelson, the cook, walks in the kitchen door with Gina, a server, right behind him.

"Hi everyone, this is Campbell, he'll be helping you out

today. Nelson, show him the ropes please, and he'll be trying to keep the dishes manageable too," I say, while Gina laughs at my joke about any kind of managing of the never ending dishes, and they both wave to Campbell.

"We'll be back shortly, but I need to steal Olivia for a little bit," my dad says and heads to the office while I trail him and my heart clenches with the air in my lungs growing thin.

It isn't strange for my dad to need to speak with me about something or another, but with Mom sick, every time he wants to talk to me in private it's scary. By the time I take a seat on the other side of the desk from where I normally am, and the office door is shut, I'm afraid I might vomit and my hands are twisted into my apron.

"Mom is okay, this isn't about that," Dad says, and I take a deep breath, releasing my grip on my apron.

"Okay, so what's up?" I ask.

"Junior is taking a break from med school," he says.

"Excuse me? What now?"

"He's thinking about returning to the restaurant and learning how to take over." Dad has the decency to look at me as he says this insane thing that rips my world apart. But he only maintains eye contact for a second before he drops his gaze to his hands, clasped against each other like he's arm wrestling himself.

"I…" My voice fails me. There is nothing to say to this. It's my parent's restaurant, it was never mine. No matter how much I want it to be mine, it isn't, and they can do with it what they want. "I'm going back to work."

He doesn't speak to me as I make my exit, out of his office, through the kitchen, and up the stairs to our apartment.

I miss the signs as I open the door. The signs that this isn't a sanctuary from my problems either.

"Hey, Livvy. What are you doing up here?" my brother calls

from the kitchen where he's making himself a sandwich with my chicken. The meat I made the other day for my own salads, something different from pizza, something light. And there he is, eating it.

"What the hell?" I scream.

CHAPTER 5

I can't. Not right now. I can't deal with him. I can't muster the energy to stop him. And I can't get past him to my room.

Damn it.

"Livvy, where are you going?" he yells, to my back as I turn and flee back down the stairs to the restaurant.

I have a whole shift ahead of me, hours more before I can reasonably beg off and have no one question me. My breath is coming in rasps and tearing through my clenched teeth into lungs that don't want the air. The world is red hot and I can't even smell the pizza anymore. I smell blood and fire. The heat normally contained to my cheeks has spread and is engulfing my body. My hands are shaking, my feet slamming against the stairs and out onto the floor of the restaurant's kitchen.

"Olivia, are you okay?" Campbell says, his mouth slightly open, his eyebrows drawn together, and his body stopped, mid stride in front of me.

A scream is building in my throat. I can't answer him. There aren't words. Tears are streaming down my face. Stupid, useless tears.

"Campbell, you go on," Dad says, "I'll handle this."

And I snap.

"Oh, you'll handle it? Like you've been handling this whole damn business? No, Dad. You haven't been handling shit. I have. And now you're going to let Junior come in here and take it all away from me, for why? Because he's a boy?" There are no spaces between my words, and I'm vaguely aware of the fact there are customers in the dining area who can probably hear my shouting, barely contained rage.

"Olivia, that's not fair, and you never wanted the restaurant," Dad says, his hands out and trying to usher me into the office.

"Don't touch me," I say, slapping his hand away, "I'm not hiding in the office so you can pretend this is okay. This isn't okay. He isn't going to do anything; he'll sit around and collect a paycheck. That's it, and you know it." My hands are in fists, my body is still as hot as the inside of an oven and I'm shaking so hard I feel like I'm vibrating.

"Come on, Olivia. My name is on the sign," my brother says from behind me.

I whirl around to see him lounging in the doorway to the stairs. He's leaning against the doorjamb still munching on a piece of my chicken.

For the first time ever in my life, I want to punch someone in the face. And for the first time ever in my life, I think my brother deserves it.

"That's my chicken," I say. The heat is leeching out of me, leaving behind an ice-covered tundra and my tears are freezing, stopping in their tracks. "I made that, it's mine. You don't get to steal from me anymore. You want to come in here after I've been doing all the work to keep us afloat and pretend like the fact you share a name with Dad means a damn thing other than our parents suck at naming sons? Listen, asshole-"

"Woah, Olivia," Dad cuts me off, putting his hand on my shoulder.

I shake my shoulder out of his grasp and understand what this icy feeling is. This is the place from which I don't care what I say to them, and I want them to hurt from my words. This is the feeling I need to eviscerate them with words.

"You both just conspired to steal my future, you don't get to *woah* me, Dad."

"What's going on?" Mom says.

Junior stands up straight and turns to where Mom is standing on the stairs behind him. Her bald head is wrapped in a scarf, her clothes covered by a fuzzy bathrobe, her arms crossed over her chest, and her jaw clenched with murder in her eyes.

"Angela, you should go back upstairs," Dad says, and mom holds her hand up in the stop motion.

"I absolutely will not. *Our* daughter just said you two conspired to steal her future? What is she talking about?" Mom says, and Dad shrinks in response.

This ought to be good.

I cross my arms over my chest and raise an eyebrow at my dad, who has the good sense to look at the floor and shut his mouth.

Junior, however, takes this opportunity to prove he's a moron.

"Olivia's being a brat, Mom. We've got this, you go back to bed," Junior says, and it's everything I can do not to laugh out loud.

"Junior, if you ever talk down to me like that again, you can expect a bill for all the things I've paid for while you've been in college," Mom says, and he drops his eyes, finally figuring out that he isn't in charge right now.

"So? Joe? Junior?" She waits, letting the pause grow uncomfortable, until my brother and my dad are visibly squirming. It is glorious.

Mom turns her eyes to mine. She may not know what's going on, but it feels like at least one member of my family is on my side right now because the murder falls out of her gaze and the corners of her mouth turn up.

"Olivia?"

"Junior seems to have decided to not be a doctor," I say, and Mom sucks in her breath, her eyes turning a withering stare onto my brother. I almost feel sorry for him. No, I don't.

Before she can start tearing him to shreds for this latest stupid idea, I barrel on, "Instead, he thinks he can walk back in here and take over the restaurant I've been running, and he's been getting paid to not work in, while Dad's been busy."

Mom looks back at me and furrows her brow.

Did she not know? Has she been that out of it? Has Dad not bothered to tell her all I've been doing while he's been taking care of her?

My mind is racing while she studies my father's downturned eyes, his slumped shoulders, and while she looks at my doofus brother, the chicken hanging limply in his hand.

"Joe, you are coming upstairs with me. Olivia, I assume you're wearing your apron because you're on shift?" Mom asks.

"Yes, Mom."

"Then, if you're okay, finish your shift. Junior, now would be a good time to show me you care at all about this business. Now would be a good time for you to follow through on your responsibilities here. You want to take over the whole running of the restaurant? Prove it. We'll finish this conversation after you're done," Mom says and starts up the stairs, clinging to the banister and testing each step she takes because the chemo has wreaked so much havoc on the nerves in her legs.

Dad scrambles to be by her side, reaching out for her so she can lean on him as she normally does. This time she takes his hand, but with the other hand she keeps her grasp on the banister and keeps leaning more on the railing than on him.

I take a deep breath and blow it through blown out cheeks while I wipe the remains of the tears from my face.

Junior doesn't look at me as he tosses the last piece of my chicken in the trash, puts on his apron, and starts scrubbing his hands in the sink.

"You can be a server for tonight. I'll bus and take the payments," I say, turning away from him to start doing my damn job. Let's see how he likes pretending it's great to be the face of the business for the night.

"Livvy," he starts, but I cut him off before he can say anything other than my name.

"No, Junior. I don't want to talk to you right now, and I don't have to. You aren't actually my boss, so go pretend like you know what you're doing in this place, and the fiftieth time you need to come check with me if we have something, if such and such is still on the menu from the summer, or if we still stock that beer, remember that you've been getting paid all this time for not knowing the answers."

I stalk away from him, past a concerned looking Campbell, and Nelson who is pointedly continuing to throw a pie, like nothing in the world just happened other than a new order came across the line.

CHAPTER 6

We are slammed that night and Junior and I don't make it off the floor until closing. He's a disaster. He screws up so often I have to break my self-imposed quarantine from the customers to smooth a few mussed feathers. But the positive comments from the customers about me in comparison to the mess my brother is, leave me buoyed for the clean up, and we get done in record time. Still, it's 2:25 am on Sunday morning by the time my brother and I head upstairs to home, and whatever reckoning is waiting for us.

I don't say a word to him. He doesn't talk to me. There really is nothing to say between us right now, no matter what he thought earlier.

Cracking open the door to the apartment, I see Mom, with her legs stretched out in front of her across the cushions, sitting on the couch.

Dad isn't in view, which is weird. He doesn't leave her up at night without him by her side.

"I want you both to sit down," Mom says.

Junior sits by her feet on the long sofa, and I sit on the

loveseat, my heart beat picking up speed. The last time my mom set up such an ominously dour chat, she went into embarrassing detail about sex. At least then my brother wasn't in the room, but whatever this is, it's drastically different and so much worse. My cramping stomach tells me I'm not going to like any of this.

"You both need to know, I wasn't aware of what's been going on and that stops now." Mom turns to Junior, her face a mask of calm and I know my brother is in real trouble. "I didn't know you were leaving med school."

Mom doesn't ask a question, she makes her statement and waits. The master interrogator is at work. Junior is a dead man.

"I didn't officially leave," he says, and my eyebrows shoot up. Oh, really?

Mom continues to wait in her stony silence. Maybe she knows, but I don't think even Dad knows most of the story based on the way Junior usually keeps everyone shut out, and if I'm right, if Dad doesn't know, Mom doesn't either. Junior, of course, doesn't think about that and try to deny anything. He just blurts what's on his mind.

"I'm not sure if I want the restaurant, or if I want to continue with med school. But I was looking at this semester and I knew I was supposed to register, and I went to the counselor and asked for a semester off instead. They didn't want to give it to me, but I told them about you," he says, and looks down at his hands folded in his lap.

Mom's back goes rigid, and I brace myself on my brother's behalf.

"You told them about my cancer, not about me," Mom says.

"Yes. I'm sorry," he says, with at least the decency to look at her while he apologizes. "I just needed a break and I thought maybe it would be great to run the restaurant. I mean, it makes good money, my name is on the sign, and I know that was Dad's original plan."

"When he made that plan your sister didn't exist," Mom says.

I want to punch him and say, yeah. But I don't.

"What do you think will happen? She'll just be happy to let you take over?" Mom asks, and she sounds genuinely curious.

She might be curious, but I can't believe this is a conversation that's actually happening because the actions that brought us here make absolutely no sense.

"I guess…" Junior says, and then glances my way before returning his gaze to his hands. "I didn't think about what Livvy would do, or how she would feel about it."

"Hmmph." Mom makes her oh-really-so-then-you-decided-to-act-a-fool sound. "And what about the money?" she asks, making me sit up straighter.

The pay he's been getting wasn't something I expected her to cover in this sit down.

"Well, I have expenses, and Dad said," Junior starts, but Mom stops him with her hand raised.

"The discussions you had with your father are irrelevant. What you did, getting a paycheck from the business without working any hours at all, instead of just asking when you needed money, wasn't okay."

"And Olivia, I wish you would have told me," Mom says, turning her piercing green eyes on me.

"I'm sorry, Mom." It's all I can say. She's right. I should have told her. I was trying to make sure she didn't stress about anything, and that's not respecting the fact that she's my mother, and plenty grown up enough to handle things, even though she's sick.

"Now, how are we going to resolve the issue of who takes over the business?" She says it as though we should come up with the answer, as if it is perfectly clear what the answer is.

I have no idea.

Junior and I don't say anything. Now that he's been

reminded that the world doesn't revolve around him, he's just as much at a loss for what to do as I am.

"What I want for you both to do, is not worry about it at this moment," Mom says, and I furrow my brow.

"I know you both think this is something that has to be hashed out right now, or preferably when you were babies, but that's not how life works. It's messy and people's plans change. Junior, you're not sure whether or not you're going back to med school. Olivia, you haven't even graduated high school yet. And Dad and I aren't yet ready to retire and move to Arizona." Mom smiles for the first time since we came upstairs, and I'm reminded of how uncertain it is she will have a retirement at all.

"I want you both to let me know when things are happening around here, especially if they're going to end in my children being at each other's throats. And extra especially if Dad is being a bonehead," Mom says, with a giggle. "I also want you to both think about what you want to do, neither of you have to take over this place. This is your father's dream; it doesn't have to be yours."

"Thanks, Mom," Junior says and moves to stand up, but she puts her hand in the air and he freezes, half way to standing.

"You are going to have to do something else," she says, and he sits back down.

"You seem to think this business is yours to exploit how you want. You draw a paycheck when you want, and work when you want, and you think you can walk in and take over something you've never spent the effort to know. That stops now. You will not be drawing a paycheck until you work off all you owe from whatever you've drawn that you haven't earned."

Junior opens his mouth and his eyes grow hard, she raises her hand again and her eyes grow murderous.

"Don't you dare argue with me. You have been spoiled your whole life, and all this time while you've been in college, we've been paying for it, no student loans for you. But that wasn't enough. You stole from a business that isn't your personal piggy bank. You should have asked us for money," Mom says, lifting one eyebrow until his clenched jaw releases and he shuts his eyes, softening the edges of him.

"Olivia, please at some point this week look through the last few months since you've been doing the bookkeeping and let me know how much he owes. Now, I'm tired, Junior; please go get your father from our room."

Junior does as he's told, and I remain sitting with the assumptions and rules of my world lying in shattered, sharp edges at my mother's feet.

"Olivia, I know you're disappointed. But I want you to take a step back, stop closing during the week, and try to figure out if this is really what you want." My mom smiles at me and holds out her arms.

I go to her and fold her into a hug, feeling the insubstantial way her bones feel through her robe. Each vertebra is clear under my hand on her back.

The truth I don't say as I hug my mother is that I would give up any future, not just the restaurant, but all my possible life directions if that's what it took to make her better.

I release her and kiss her on the cheek to make my hasty exit to my room, so she doesn't see my tears.

CHAPTER 7

$\mathcal{I}$'m bored. Dear lord, how do people not do anything? My homework is done. I've already eaten dinner.

The noise from the restaurant, a dull hum in my room upstairs, does nothing but remind me that I could be, should be, down in the restaurant.

Mom's edict seems impossible to follow, and I'm only two days in. The lack of friends is becoming a glaring empty space in my life. I don't think I even have anyone's number besides Theresa, and I am not desperate enough to bored dial my ex. My phone sits on my desk as unused as always. It's only there for emergencies really. The majority of the numbers I have in it are for people connected to the restaurant.

This is pathetic. I am pathetic. I have discovered I have no hobbies. My room is just a place I have my bed.

Even the amazing turret that peaks over my bed, the intricate ceiling I'm staring at, does nothing to inspire me and would do nothing to tell anyone anything about me. Everything is tidy, even my desk. Everything is in its place. My furniture and decorations are from five years ago. I don't even like the color of my bedding anymore.

Lilac? Yuck. I want burgundy. Something deep and rich, like the brown of Omar's eyes.

I sit up and look around my room. At the framed poems I liked so many years ago. At the books I haven't bothered to freshen up in so long.

Something in me gives in to my mother. Okay, so I need to make some changes. But that doesn't mean throwing out the recipe because I burnt the first pizza.

I can do both.

A notebook from my desk I had been planning on using for the next few months of schedules for shifts in the restaurant becomes my game plan.

Every day during the week I'll work, not close, but put in some time. No one does anything social during the week anyway. I'll still be following Mom's rules, and not bored out of my mind.

Meanwhile, I'll try to connect with people at school and on the weekends. I'll take the opening and lunch shifts on the weekends so I'm still not closing and following Mom's grand plan. And I've already handed over all the paperwork portions of the restaurant to my dad.

I suspect he's trying to get Junior to do it, and that I'll have to step in to save him at some point, but for now I'll let them try and do everything without me and my proverbial red cape.

First, though, I need to make some changes in my material world. On my list goes all the things I would like to replace in my room. My desk, for sure.

Staring at my desk makes me realize it's just a junky old child's desk. I need a real one. Big and solid wood with more storage than I think I'll need. A file cabinet, a bookshelf, and a comfortable desk chair all go on my list too.

The walls around me are mocking me, because I have no idea what to do about them. I have two pictures on my wall over my desk. One of me and my mom when she first lost her hair and I wore a bald cap. And one of our whole family just a month before she first got diagnosed. The only other thing on my walls are the framed poems. I don't know art. I don't know what I would like for art in my own room. The emptiness of my idea tank for them is daunting, so I focus on other things.

I can order a new bed. I can order a rug. I can order new bedding.

Wait. No, I can't. I have money saved, but it needs to stay there in case Mom needs it for her treatment, or the restaurant does for something. And it needs to stay in case Junior gets the restaurant and I have to start a completely different life than the one I thought I would live.

My list would be expensive if I tried to do all of it.

The desk I can look for second hand, that will help. Everything else for that side of my room can wait.

But bedding. Bedding and a new rug. I don't need to replace my whole bed yet, but it would make my room look vastly different if I just do these two relatively cheap things.

With the hum of the restaurant below me, I get online and start shopping, something I never have time to do.

The bedding I find is beautiful and rich, the rug reflecting the same style. I'm finding exactly what makes me happy on my screen and tamp down my instinct to feel guilty about it.

See, Mom? I'm finding a balance like you wanted already.

Tomorrow it's time to try and make friends.

CHAPTER 8

I storm into the restaurant after school and slam the door of the office after I throw my stuff inside. Looking up from where I'm yanking on the ties to my apron, I spot Campbell.

He's frozen with his eyebrows high and a stack of plates he's putting away stopped in the air in his outstretched hand.

"Okay," I say out loud, taking a deep breath and reminding myself that school is over. I can forget all about today.

"Sorry, Campbell," I say to him as I adjust the now too tight ties of my apron.

He puts away the stack of plates and then moves toward me, ducked around the corner from the view of the dining room.

"Are you okay?" he asks, quiet, but there is sincerity in his eyes, genuine concern.

"Yeah, it's just a strange time. Don't worry about me. How's it been here?" I ask him, leaning against the wall to give myself an extra few seconds to prepare for customers being right only in theory.

"Um," Campbell darts his eyes toward the corner and the end of the kitchen open to the dining room.

"What?"

"Well, Junior is, uh, not you," he says, and I laugh.

"I don't know if that's a good thing or a bad thing," I say.

"It's not great," he says. His voice is grave, low and weighty, like I shouldn't be laughing this off.

"I'll be right back," I say, and head around the corner.

The dining rooms near the kitchen are weirdly empty for this time of the day. The afternoon crowd usually likes to be by the kitchen to see the dough tossed.

I walk into the next area of the dining room and realize why Campbell seemed so serious.

My idiot brother is looming over two tables simultaneously that are full of girls. They aren't happy about it. One girl closest to him is fully turned away from him, giving Junior her back. Another girl is staring daggers, and the rest are various shades of pissed off and uncomfortable.

Meanwhile the other patrons are sitting at their tables with their menus or their empty cups in hand trying to get his attention.

"Junior," I call to him and he straightens.

He turns to me with one eyebrow raised like I'm the one that deserves questioning right now and walks toward me, still ignoring the other customers. One of whom almost slams his menu down on the table in front of him.

"Aren't you supposed to be taking a break," he asks when he gets to me.

"Aren't you supposed to be working and not flirting? How long have they been waiting for you to take their order?" I ask and head to the tables with menus first.

I have to run interference, apologize, and clean up Junior's mistakes more than do my own work all night.

With each new way he invents to utterly screw up, my determination that my brother not be in charge of the restaurant grows. There is no way this is his calling. It would close in a matter of a few years. I won't let that happen. And we can't be in the business together. I would kill him. Somehow, I have to find a way to prove to my parents that I'm the one who should take over, and he should either go back to med school or find something else to do.

I start formulating ideas of how to prove my point to my parents just as I notice him heading toward the wrong table with a pizza.

He needs to do literally anything else.

"Junior, only one person orders anchovy, ever. That goes to table twelve," I say as he passes me.

For his part, he doesn't argue or give me a dirty look or anything. He turns and heads to table twelve with a smile still on his face.

I shake my head and go back to the kitchen with my tray full of dirty dishes.

Campbell is waiting at the sink for me.

"You said he was in med school," Campbell says, looking to my brother taking out the last order of the night to an alcove table. He sounds skeptical, and, honestly, I can't blame him after Junior's performance tonight.

"He's actually brilliant," I say, and Campbell scoffs while he turns back to the dishes. "Junior just doesn't bother to put any effort into anything he deems beneath him." I say and lean against the edge of the sink to rub the back of my neck. It's exhausting to be this person who makes everything better for everyone else. I thought it was hard before, but this is worse. At least before it was done right the first time.

"Your brother thinks your incredible family legacy is

beneath him?" Campbell asks, his mouth hanging slightly open and eyes wide, distracted from his task.

"Well, he's a genius; I never said he was smart," I say and leave him, laughing, to his work while I go make sure my brother doesn't screw anything else up.

A half hour later I lock the door behind the last customers to leave, refusing to follow Mom's edict not to close.

When I turn around, I find the dining area empty. I clean the tables and mop the floor, waiting for my brother to come help me, but he doesn't. Campbell does.

By the time I'm finished with the floor and moving on to count out the till, Campbell comes from the kitchen to start stocking the bussing stations.

"Is Junior in the office?" I ask.

Campbell pops his head around the edge of one of the stations to say, "No, he went upstairs."

"He what?"

"Uh, he went upstairs," Campbell says, grimacing.

I'm sure he can tell how not okay that is. I rub the back of my neck and let it go so I can focus on counting out.

None of this is my fault or my problem. This is Junior's fault and Mom and Dad's problem. But it's so hard to listen to my mom and not try and take care of this. Especially because it feels like telling them would be some kind of tattle-tale move on my part. Maybe they would take it as me not telling the truth to prove I should inherit.

So maybe I can't let it go. The count is done, I bag up the deposit and put it in the safe in the office. Passing through the kitchen I find that Campbell has already done all the closing chores in here too.

Closing the door of the office behind me I look up in time to see Campbell throwing his apron in the laundry bin.

"Hey, Campbell, I want to thank you for working so hard," I say.

"Olivia, you already tipped me out," he says, with a laugh and I smile.

"No, I mean it. It's nice that you're always working so hard, and always willing to chip in," I say and shrug.

It may sound silly to him. It's his job, but he goes above and beyond and seems to genuinely care about the restaurant after not being here very long. It isn't silly to me, it matters to me, and I just want to let him know.

"I like it here," he says, grabbing his coat out of his locker.

"Olivia, if there's any way I can help with anything, let me know okay?" he says and reaches for the door.

He's pulling it open before a thought pops into my head, an out there thought, and one I never believed I would have, but Mom wants me to find balance.

"Drastic," I say, and he stops, turning to look at me with his eyebrows raised in a question.

"You said I need to do something drastic. Mom says I need to get a life outside this place and I'm starting to wonder if maybe a life would mean she would agree to give me the restaurant," I say and take a few steps in his direction, staring at the floor because this is even more awkward than I normally am.

"They're really questioning which one of you should get this place? They're being stupid."

"Yeah, well, stupid or not, I think maybe that a not date outing or two would be a good idea," I say, croaking out my words through a throat so nervous it wants to slam shut.

"What are you doing tomorrow?" he asks, and my eyes snap up to meet his.

He's grinning that half grin and my cheeks heat with a blush that only makes his smile grow to both sides of his mouth.

"I have school," I say, at a loss for what I do next, for where we go from here.

"Okay, I'll pick you up from school at the end of the day. We'll take Omar and a couple other people out somewhere. Do you have to come back here?" he asks.

I look down at my feet while my cheeks burn at how horribly weird this is, at how horribly awkward tomorrow could be. Am I ready for this? My hands are shaking.

Campbell takes my shaking hands in his and I look up at him where he stands directly in front of me now.

"It's okay," he says.

"I don't have to work tomorrow if I don't want to, but I'm not sure I can pull this off," I say, begging him in my mind to understand.

His hands squeeze mine and he reaches up to tuck a piece of my hair behind my ear. The gesture is something my mother does, and its familiar feel helps to ease the shaking.

"We're just going in a group to have some fun. I'll be there to help. You're not alone in this," he says, with a soft smile and I take a deep breath as my shaking stops.

CHAPTER 9

It's just a group going to do something. I keep repeating it in my head all through the day at school. At lunch I sit at my normal table with the rest of the socially awkward kids and don't say a word. In classes I barely hear what's going on around me. By the time I'm heading out to the parking lot five minutes before the last bell because when a student who never gets in trouble for anything asks a teacher to leave early to get home and help their mom, the teacher obliges, my hands are shaking again.

The doors to school are heavy as I push them open and I spot Campbell easily, leaning against his car. My shaking slows and I marvel at him as I walk his way. He's graceful even standing there. Like he belongs wherever he is, and among the angles and lines of the harsh metal on all the cars around him, his softer edges of the lines of his body makes for a beautiful, instead of clashing, contrast.

"Hey, Olivia," he says as I get closer and he smiles, my shaking completely disappearing as he does.

"I was nervous, so I wanted to get out here before anyone else did," I say.

"Well, they're not riding with us, so we can get an even bigger head start on them and head out if you want," he says and opens the passenger door of the car for me.

"You know, that's awfully chivalrous for a non-date," I say, but climb in as he laughs.

He darts around the car to jump into the driver's side and starts the engine.

"You keep calling it a non-date, but it's a fake date so we need to act like it."

"Well, you're doing a good job so far," I say.

"So, if this was a real date you would have been happy to leave school early and take off with no idea where you were headed?" he asks, turning down a street near the restaurant.

"As long as we're not going to my house, then, yeah."

"We are not going to the restaurant. I know you well enough to know if we went there you wouldn't be able to stop yourself from stepping in and working instead of being able to relax," he says, shaking his head.

"You know that about me already?"

"Olivia, I figured that out about you my first day of work," he says, lifting one eyebrow and smiling with half his mouth at me while we stop at a light.

"Ugh. I really am a workaholic, aren't I?" I ask, turning to look back at him and smiling.

The car behind us honks and we both look forward to the now green light.

"Sorry," he says, as I laugh.

"So, what is the grand plan for tonight, and how late are we going to be out?" I ask.

"The plan is to force everyone to be as ridiculous as possible and thereby eliminating any of your nerves, and we'll only stay out a couple hours. I don't want to get on the wrong side of your parents by keeping you out so late you don't have time to do your homework," he says and winks at me.

I shake my head at him and sit back in the car. He's magic, because I'm more relaxed than I was when I fell asleep last night.

That is until he pulls into the parking lot of Seattle's Best Karaoke.

"Seriously?" I ask, and I want to jump out of the car and sprint down the sidewalk away from here.

"Come on, Olivia. Everyone will be so nervous and bad at it that it won't matter if you are. This is a great idea," he says, prying one of my hands off the car door handle and holding it firmly between his.

"I'm going to suck at this," I say, and he smiles a reassuring smile at me, small and understanding. It doesn't really help.

"You don't understand. I can't stand in front of a room full of people and sing," I say, my voice quaking.

"In there, you won't have to," he says. "Trust me, okay?"

Looking at him, so earnest and sure, I decide to try for trust. So far, he hasn't done anything but try and look out for me or help me. I drag a deep breath in, and steel myself for whatever happens inside a business whose name may as well be torture chamber.

"Please don't let this kill me," I say. And he smiles.

He lets go of my hand and gets out of the car, I climb from my side and we walk into the building.

Inside is non-descript, almost like the lobby of a doctor's office. I can only hear murmurs from the many doors off the hallway past the front desk. The sounds coming from the doors are as if televisions are on inside the rooms, but I would never be able to tell what channel the people inside are watching, they're too quiet.

None of this is what I was expecting. Campbell talks to the man behind the counter as I look around, trying to figure out where the stage is, where the crowd of people watching the poor sap making a fool of themselves is.

"Olivia, this way," Campbell says, and I follow him down the hall to a door marked with a number like in a hotel.

He opens the door to a room with no windows and a couple couches facing a television and sound system on a table with shelves below that are filled to bursting with binders.

"What is this place?" I ask and take a seat on one of the very new couches.

"Seattle's Best is all like this, private karaoke rooms. I ordered us a bunch of snacks and drinks too," he says, running his finger along the spines of the binders below the TV.

"How do you know about this place?" Is all I can think to ask in this weird reality where a place like this even exists.

"When I was a kid, we came to Seattle to visit Omar and his family, and we came here. That was before the virus," he says.

And I know what he means. The whole world measures time by before and after the virus. In some places it got ugly; the worst of humanity came out, not in Seattle even though we were hit especially hard. My hometown responded to it the way it does to most things: by becoming more supportive of each other, we responded with more love, not less.

"The restaurant became delivery during the virus. Dad just kept on cooking, and dropping off tons of meals to the local shelters," I say, thinking how it's a minor miracle none of us got sick, and how it's a small consolation that Mom didn't have cancer in the middle of it. We wouldn't have been able to do what we did.

"The Dominican eventually shut everything down. Even with the help from the government, for an island reliant on tourism it was..." he trails off and doesn't finish his thought.

He doesn't have to. I can hear it in his voice; the surrealness, the hardship.

"Okay, so no more of that. We need to get you started picking some songs," he smiles, and the spell is broken. We're back to this moment, this time, this much smaller version of scary.

"Do we really need to?" I ask, as the door opens and Omar, Theresa, two other cheerleaders, and one more football player crowd into the room in a noisy, chattering group.

"Hey, Olivia, Campbell, we ready for this? We all had to beg stomach issues to get out of practice," Omar says, sitting on the coffee table.

I pop up from the couch and go to Campbell standing by the TV while everyone makes their way to snag the seats, Omar claiming an arm of the big couch so he isn't sitting on the coffee table that is the only surface I can see for the snacks Campbell said he ordered.

There's only one seat left and I'm staring at it as they talk about how pissed off the football and cheerleading coach will be if they find out none of them actually have food poisoning.

"Coach probably thinks we all went to a party last night and can't hold our liquor," Deacon, the other football player says, his voice deep and thrumming which makes me think he'll do just fine at this.

"Only five of us? No, they won't suspect a thing," Theresa says and glances at me with the shy smile I used to find delicious and now makes me a little sad.

The man from the front desk walks in with a tray of snacks, mostly fried finger foods, and a pitcher of Coke.

"Thank you," goes up in a discordant chorus and I realize we should not try any ensemble pieces.

"Okay, who's up first?" Campbell asks as he pours me a cup and tosses a mozzarella stick into his mouth.

"I am; let's get this started right," Omar says, grabbing for the binders.

Campbell comes to my side with my drink and I realize how awkward we are just standing here while everyone else looks through the books for songs they want. But there's only one seat left, and I don't want to be that girl and take it.

I look up at Campbell, my stomach starting to turn itself inside out, and he smiles at me and takes my hand. He leans down to whisper in my ear, "Fake date needs to look real, remember."

My cheeks heat and I cover my smile with my cup, so the rest of the room doesn't catch on through my face that something is up.

Campbell leads me over to the couch and the last seat, sitting in it himself before pulling me down to perch on his lap.

My face is on fire, but looking up through my lashes I see Theresa staring with her mouth hanging open and Omar looking at us with his eyebrows way up.

I have to admit to myself, it's kind of fun to see them react. Campbell keeps a hold of my hand and his long, elegant fingers rub gently on the back if it, calming some of my blush and allowing me to forget to be embarrassed about how public this fake PDA is.

"Have you found your song yet?" Campbell asks Omar, who holds up a binder in triumph and grabs the remote, keying in a number on the screen in answer.

"Baby Got Back", which is almost a Seattle anthem comes pouring from the speakers, and it's the perfect choice.

All of us forget to be anything but having fun while we sing along, the girls alone doing the beginning, and then everyone in unison, knowing every word by heart, doing the rest.

CHAPTER 10

"*D*amn, Olivia," Omar yells while they all cheer when I'm finished with the song Campbell insisted I sing. "That was amazing; why aren't you in choir again?" he asks.

My face flames red and Campbell pulls me into a hug.

"Told you Melissa Etheridge was perfect for your voice," he says.

"I've heard that song maybe once in my life; you couldn't have found something I know?" I ask and scoot in next to him on the couch.

Now that we're all getting up to sing the seating situation has become less a case of not enough room and more one of musical chairs, a game that never manages to separate me from Campbell.

"Melissa is an original queen, so no. I wanted to hear you sing it."

"Oh, so that's why. Not because of my voice, but because you personally wanted that song. Why haven't you sung anything?" I'm whispering now while Theresa butchers a recent pop song and everyone laughs with her.

At least she knows she's terrible and jumps right in anyway, making the best joke of the situation. I'm pretty sure she's tone deaf.

"I love music, but um, my voice has trouble regulating when I sing still," he says in my ear.

Oh. I'm stupid.

"It can't be worse than her," I whisper back and am rewarded with a chuckle that shakes my side leaning against him.

His arm wraps around my back and it's nice. This version of socializing I can get behind.

We spend a couple hours taking turns on songs, Campbell my ever present anxiety blanket, and I realize he's a genius. This situation, the equal opportunity for embarrassment, is exactly the right way to get me comfortable with people.

"Olivia, we can bring in outside snacks; next time you should bring them from your restaurant," Deacon, the other football player says.

I laugh and think, next time. That's cool. He wants there to be a next time for me hanging out with them.

"Speaking of the restaurant, I've got to get Olivia home," Campbell says as he stands and pulls me to my feet.

"No, come on guys, stay. This is fun," Betty, one of the cheer-leaders says.

"Betty, it's okay. They clearly need some time alone," Theresa says, and takes the remote from Omar's hands to key in her own song choice as if he's given up his turn.

Maybe he has; his face is blank and staring at us as we say goodbye and head out the door.

"Well, that was," Campbell starts once we're in the hallway, but I cut him off.

"Weird."

"It was not. That went great," he says, taking my hand again.

"By great, do you mean the look Omar was giving us as we

left?" I ask while we shove open the door together to head to the car.

"Yeah, part of it. He's thinking, just like you want him to. Aw, shit," he says as he walks into a wall of water.

Rain is pouring down from the sky, not falling, not sprinkling, it's a torrential downpour. We're inches from the sheets of water coming down, barely protected by the roof's overhang above us. The splash from the weather hitting the ground is soaking through the calves of my jeans.

"Hang here for a second. I'll get the car unlocked so you don't have to stand in the rain waiting," Campbell says and darts out from under the roof to run to his car.

I turn to huddle closer to the building but out of the way of the door should it open, and there's a poster with a picture of a slice of pepperoni barely hanging on to the side of the building. It says, best pizza in Seattle competition. I tear off the last two pieces of tape holding it in place and hug it to my body, my mind spinning. Behind me the car horn honks, and I dart through the rain to Campbell waiting for me.

He pops open the door from the inside and I jump in, pulling it shut behind me.

"Does this happen a lot?" Campbell asks, laughing as he wipes the rain from his face.

I'm as soaked through as he is, but I pay little attention beyond just wiping the water out of my eyes so I can see the poster, damp and spotted with droplets no matter how closely I held it against my torso as I ran.

"This could work," I say out loud, completely distracted by the paper in front of me as more drops spatter onto it, falling from my hair.

"What could work?" Campbell asks and reaches out to tuck my sodden hair behind my ear.

"This. Look at this." I'm too loud in the tight confines of the car, but I can't contain how excited I am as I shove the poster at him.

He takes it from me and furrows his brow as he looks it over.

"I can do this, Campbell. I can do this, win this competition, and prove to my parents that I'm the one who should be taking over the restaurant. No matter what name is on the sign, that place should be mine. It's all I've ever known and all I've ever wanted to do," I say.

"This says a new pizza recipe," he says, reading the listing.

"Yeah. It's perfect. I know pizza," I say, pawing at my now irritating wet hair as it continues to want to dangle in my face and get in the way of this conversation.

"Of course, you do, but a whole new recipe?" He looks at me with a soft smile.

In that smile I see doubt. Of me, or this plan, I'm not sure, but it burns. I've allowed myself to get too close to him, to trust him. I've become careless and gotten too close to the oven only to walk away singed.

"Just take me home," I say, sitting back in my seat and staring out the windshield, determined to be done with this… whatever it is, with him. Friendship? Well, as close as I usually get to one.

His finger is on my chin, it's chilled and damp from the rain in contrast to the heat burning through my face I know means I'm blushing. A slight, insistent pressure from his finger turns my face toward him, away from the safety of the view out the window.

"Olivia," he says, soft and low.

Those eyes of his, their depths hide whatever he's thinking from me, but they're beautiful in the glow from the streetlights outside, muted as they are by the rain.

"I have no doubt you can do this. I have no doubt the restaurant should be yours, you know that. I have no doubt you can win, but I also think this is not going to be easy," he says, his hand still touching my face.

I open my mouth to say something and shut it again as he continues.

"But this is going to take a lot of time and effort; the competition is in two months. I just worry you'll think this is the only way to prove to your parents you want to take over, and you'll kill yourself trying. When are you going to work on this? You're so busy already." He rubs his thumb over my cheek to wipe away more water, tucking my unruly hair again, and then drops his hand to settle on mine where I rest it on the seat beside me.

What he's said chases itself around in my brain, trying to settle the feelings roiling inside me. There's hope, fear, dissipating anger and disappointment, excitement, and something else I can't catch as it flies past.

"So, you think I can do this?" I ask. Trying to focus on my hope instead of any of the other things fighting for dominance inside me.

"Yes."

There's no qualifier about his answer, it doesn't come with a seasoning of doubt, and my heart soars in excitement. I can feel a grin spreading across my face, impossible to contain now.

"In fact," he says, handing the poster back to me and starting the car, "I'm going to help you do this thing."

CHAPTER 11

The next day at school, I'm distracted in my first four classes, barely aware of what the teachers are saying and the assignments I need to take note of for homework. My mind is one thousand percent focused on the competition and what pizza I'm going to make.

I didn't lie when I told Campbell that I know pizza. I've had every kind of crust and topping combination over the years, including anchovy. But that makes thinking of a new pizza, an original, far more difficult than I anticipated while soggy in Campbell's car.

The lists of ideas I have going in my notebook are increasingly stupid. Pickles? No. Apples and sausage? Hard pass.

By the time I get to the lunchroom, I'm barely aware of my surroundings and it takes until I'm halfway across the room headed to my usual table for me to hear my name being called from my right.

I turn toward the person calling for me, and it's Omar.

"Hey, I thought for a minute you didn't hear me. Come over here and sit with us," he says, waving me over.

Okay, this is new. I guess operation make connections at school is a big win. Campbell will be thrilled.

I walk across to the boisterous table full of football players and cheerleaders and for a second, I have an out of body experience. Sure, I know all the people at the table, and all their pizza orders, but as friendly as I have been with all of them, we've never been friends. Well, except Theresa who is smiling at me as I take a seat across from her.

"Hi," she says. "I was just telling everyone how good you were last night. That song was amazing, like it was meant for your voice."

Others are nodding their heads, and my face heats up.

"Please don't ask for an encore," I say, looking down at my plate and picking at a French fry. But they laugh, and it isn't at me, it's because they think what I said was funny, I can tell by the way they poke at each other like they're daring each other to sing instead. I smile and lift my face. I can do this.

"Seriously, you should think about joining the choir," Deacon says.

"Oh, sure, so I can be so embarrassed I sing to my feet the whole time I'm on stage blushing; no, thanks," I say and laugh when he smiles and shakes his head at me.

"Why didn't your girlfriend sing?" Betty asks and I freeze with a fry halfway to my mouth.

"Boyfriend," Omar says, his voice harsh. "Campbell is Olivia's boyfriend."

Yeah, damn it.

I think. And then catch myself. My fake boyfriend.

"Oh, shit. I knew that, I'm sorry," she says, and looks genuinely contrite, but it still causes an ache in my chest.

"Campbell just wanted to sit last night out. And he can do whatever he wants," I say, heavy emphasis on he, and pop my fry into my mouth before I say something really nasty.

"I think he's hot," Katie says, and I choke on my fry.

Omar laughs at me and pounds me on the back to clear the food from my throat.

"Um, thanks?" I choke out when I can talk and Katie smiles at me.

"Seriously. If you ever get tired of him, send him to me," she says, wiggling her eyebrows at me.

I crack up laughing. Katie, I decide, I like.

"Although, I doubt that will ever happen," Deacon says.

My eyebrows furrow together, waiting for something ugly to come out of his mouth and for me to have to slap this giant guy.

"Olivia isn't stupid," he says, taking a bite out of his burger and talking with his mouth full. "That guys got it bad, and I'm sure she knows it." He looks at me and winks.

The heat blazing up my face is unstoppable. Maybe Campbell is too good an actor.

"It's a big bonus her family makes great food. Now, if I could find a girl who had a family seafood restaurant? Hoo, I would do anything for her," he says and I can barely stay upright I'm laughing so hard.

"Deacon, you are the embodiment of that old saying about a way to a man's heart," Theresa says, shaking her head. "It would be irritating if you weren't so pure."

"I am pure. That's true," he says, taking another bite of his burger while the whole table laughs.

The rest of lunch goes well, and the time spent with these people, these friends, feels like a respite from my distractions and concerns. And I learn that Deacon really is every bit the impossible to be irritated with decent dude Theresa proclaimed him to be. I also learn Katie and I are going to be good friends if she can stand me. But the thing I'm thinking about by the end of the day is the moment that didn't really register at the time.

When I'm walking out the doors of the school and heading down the sidewalk for my walk home, I realize Deacon gave me a very real gift.

He said he would do anything for a girl with a restaurant of his favorite food. I've been thinking about creating a new pizza all wrong. It isn't about new toppings necessarily. It's about creating a pizza based on a favorite food that isn't usually associated with pizza.

By the time my feet hit the sidewalk by the road, I'm walking so fast I probably look like I'm being chased by something. What I'm actually doing is chasing a damn good idea home.

CHAPTER 12

I sprint up the exterior stairwell of my apartment and fling the door open, chasing it down when the knob slips out of my hand to catch it before it slams into the wall. I shut the door behind me and in a flurry of kicking off my shoes and pulling off my back pack and coat as fast as I can, I dart into my bedroom.

My pile of stuff gets flung into the corner while I grab my notebook and start making a list of all of my favorite non-pizza related dishes. Then I make a list of my favorite ingredients, hoping it will spark a way for me to narrow my focus on one or two of the favorite recipe list, because it is far too long.

Saffron. That's it. I can put saffron in the dough and make the sauce and toppings into a paella pizza. Oh, my god. It would be amazing.

But do we even have any saffron? It's so damn expensive...

Okay, make a list of the ingredients. I scribble madly, thinking of some of the seafood Mom usually includes that would never work on a pizza because they would just make it too soggy. Not those, but clams? Calamari? Yes, to both.

My handwriting is an illegible scrawl, so I take some deep breaths, slow down and start my list over again. I have to gather everything I'm going to need and work in the morning on Saturday, earlier than I usually do even, so I'll have time to do it with all the other things I have to prep before opening.

I don't want my parents or Junior to know what I'm doing until right before. And Junior definitely can't find out until after I register for the contest online. I've kept the poster with me in my backpack so he can't see it. It may be petty to want to register as a representative of Joe's and to not allow Junior to swoop in and do it instead, especially since I don't know that he would actually even try to enter, but I don't care if it's petty or not. I will be the queen of petty if it gets Junior to go away and leave the restaurant alone.

CHAPTER 13

Saturday morning at 4:00 AM, my alarm goes off.

There is nothing I want less than to get out of bed right now. I need sleep; in a week I've grown to enjoy getting real sleep from not closing every night. Last night I worked until one in the morning, and passed out hard the minute I got into bed. I'm still wearing my shirt of the night before, although I did manage to get out of my jeans.

I peel my eyes open as wide as I can get them to go and hit the alarm clock, silencing the unholy torture device. I have to get up. There's so much to do.

My legs don't want to listen when I tell them to move, to swing down to the floor.

Damn it, we have work to do. I'm yelling at my own legs in my head, but it works. I finally get up and wander into the bathroom for a shower. There is zero possibility I'll make it today if I don't take a shower.

I get under the water before it gets up to temperature, it helps wake me up the rest of the way. My shampoo smells like some generic floral, and it makes me wonder what the good products Campbell uses are.

He said he would help me with the competition, but this morning is about me and my research muscles getting a work out. I've got to source all the ingredients I'll need. Since we have never had a pizza with any seafood as a topping, I'm not sure my current suppliers will be able to get me anything. And I'm hoping beyond hope that because I'm not buying in bulk, they won't charge me too much. If they are too expensive, or their minimum order is too large, it will be me and Pike Place Market getting to know each other better.

Done with my shower, I turn off the water, my towel is warm from hanging above the heat register waiting for me. This is the best feeling normally, but right now it makes me want to crawl back into my bed and remain cozy.

I don't, of course. I get dressed and pull my hair back, put some concealer under my eyes to cover up the purple bruise looking areas that mark me so clearly as someone who should not be awake yet. Finishing up with some mascara and gloss makes me feel like I look ready for the day, even if I'm not.

My house isn't awake yet, and Mom, Dad, and Junior won't be up for a while, so I tiptoe to the kitchen and make myself a bowl of little kids frosted cereal. There are healthier options in the pantry, but sugar is what I crave right now.

Something needs to jolt my system into not just moving about, but actually functioning.

The restaurant is dark, the sun not yet up to brighten it through the windows, and for the first time in a long time I wonder about the rumor that this place was haunted before Mom and Dad bought it.

Well, if there are ghosts in the building, they must like what we've done with the place, because they've never been a problem. I don't bother to turn on the lights, I just make my way in the dark to the door of the office. In there, though, I finally flip a light switch.

My notebook with my plans in it is where I left it, tucked under the order book, which makes me wonder if Junior bothered to do the order this week.

It doesn't matter. Mom and Dad wanted me to step back, I remind myself. I need to let Junior crash and burn if that's what needs to happen. I can't come flying in to save the day until Mom and Dad know he's botched it all. But I don't want to wait.

Fingers itching to call up the orders on the computer, I have to sit on my hands and take deep breaths before I set the book aside and focus on this task, this competition, and all I need it to do for me.

My notebook has the numbers of our suppliers in it, and I start making calls. The hours slip by unnoticed as my task for the day slips from doing something I need done, to patching up problems Junior and Dad have caused. A missed payment to one, missed orders to all.

Before I stop myself and overthink things, I send a group text to Mom, Dad, and Junior. This is ridiculous, if they let this continue, we will be out of business. If a global pandemic wasn't enough to close us down, I'll be damned if my idiot brother will do it.

Imagine my surprise when I come to the office and call some of our suppliers to work on a personal project and find that not only has a payment been missed, but the orders haven't been placed yet this week. We are now paying extra for rushed and over large orders because we will be out of half our ingredients before their regular deliveries. Remind me again how I'm supposed to be stepping back?

Maybe it's too harsh. I don't care anymore. One of them is going to have to actually do something. I suspect Dad has grown so used to me doing everything, knowing all the things that need to be done, he doesn't even bother to remind Junior. If I find out either of them pawn things off on Mom and expect her to be the one to pick up all my duties, I might explode.

How am I supposed to do the things Mom wants me to? How am I supposed to get this competition won for the restaurant if I'm doing everything still?

I drop my face into my hands, a few tears sneaking out to dampen my fingers.

"Hey, are you okay?" Campbell asks from the doorway.

Pulling my hands away from my face, I wipe the stupid angry tears in the process and hope he doesn't see.

"I'm just tired," I say. It isn't entirely a lie, so I don't feel my face flood with the heat of a blush. I learned a long time ago that the only way around my stupid face while lying was to not lie, tell mostly the truth and my face can't betray me.

"Why are you down here now? Wait, did you get an idea for the competition?" Campbell asks, and his face brightens, his smile wide.

"Yes, and no." I get up from behind the desk and skirt around him in the doorway, heading to put on my apron.

"What does yes and no mean?" he asks, as I peak over at the overflowing laundry bin.

"Well, I have an idea for a recipe, but the best price I could find for one of the ingredients is four thousand for a kilo," I say, shoving the bin toward the laundry alcove.

"Let me help, Olivia. Then you can explain to me why you need a whole kilo of something that costs as much as the car I'm looking at." He darts around me to open the washer and starts throwing aprons in.

"You're looking at buying a car? I thought you had one." I grab the detergent down from the shelf and pour it in while he finishes shoving the last of the ties in and shuts the door of the washer.

"I've been borrowing my aunt's car; I need to have my own though because the bus system here kind of sucks," he says, grabbing the bin and pushing it back to its place, while I start the load.

"The bus system does suck, especially if you want to go anywhere outside of Seattle. If you want to cross into another county, good luck. Do you have enough parking at your place? If not, you can leave it in the back lot when you don't need it," I say, washing up to get ready for the prep.

"Thanks, but yeah, we have enough. There isn't room for any friends to park, but city parking is the same no matter what country you're in: tough." He washes up with me, passing the towel to dry our hands off afterward.

"By the way, you can't change the subject forever." He bumps his arm into mine and smiles.

"Not forever, I just needed to think about something not food related for a minute." I smile back and we get to grabbing all of our ingredients and items for prepping.

"So, it's been a minute. Hit me with your brilliant plan," he says.

"Okay, so, do you like paella?" I ask, and he blinks a few times before answering.

"Yes, but what does that have to do with pizza?"

"At first I was going about it all wrong, but I realized that almost any of your favorite dishes can be turned into a pizza if you're creative enough and worrying more about the flavor profile." I'm talking while I'm getting dough ready, and I realize I'm getting too excited and I have to consciously slow my hands, so I don't screw up.

"Not everything works though; there have been some really gross attempts from local places back home." He shivers and twists his face up in disgust while I laugh.

"True, so I need to be able to have enough time and ingredients to try different things out and see what does and doesn't work. Hence, the kilo of one of the most important ingredients of paella, saffron," I say, and his eyebrows raise.

"Saffron is that expensive?" he asks, his hands frozen mid chop.

"Yeah, the good stuff costs a fortune, and that's actually a great price I only got because of my connections. I plan on putting it in the dough. Can you imagine? Oh, the crust would be heaven." My mouth waters a bit just thinking about it and I realize I haven't eaten enough today. That cereal is long gone; I need to get something in me before customers arrive.

"The crust would be really good, yeah, but it doesn't cost nearly that much in the Dominican Republic. I think you're being taken," he says, shaking his head and getting back to work.

"Okay, can you get me some from the Dominican, because that would be amazing and maybe then I could afford it, because right now it's hard for me to make the case that it's even a good idea to spend that kind of money on it," I say, punching the dough in front of me and setting it aside.

"Sure, it takes a bit for mail from there usually. Like a few weeks, but I'll get my mom to send some." He smiles at me and a weight lifts.

"Wow, that… thanks," I say, smiling back, and start on another batch of dough.

"You were really stressing about the price, huh?" he asks, grabbing the dough I'm done with and taking them to the walk in.

"Of course, I kept thinking I would have to find some in a specialty shop around here, but that wouldn't really give me much wiggle room to add more to the dough recipe if I needed to." I say, feeling less tired than I did just minutes ago.

"Not to mention it would leave me with less to play with for the whole pizza. I mean, I think I'll need at least ten different tests to know if a recipe is a good idea even, let alone if it will win."

"Ten?" he asks, his voice high and scared sounding.

I look up at him to find his eyes wide and mouth agape.

"Did you think I would win a pizza contest by throwing the regular dough, regular sauce, some prosciutto and peaches on top?" I ask, he seems way too shocked for this, I mean, he said himself it would be hard.

"Well, I mean, I thought you would make a few different kinds of pizzas with unique toppings and pick one, I thought the hardest part would be thinking of toppings…" he trails off as I laugh a cold, harsh laugh.

"So what, exactly, were you warning me was going to be so hard when we were in the car? Do you really think a little savory and a little sweet would be hard for me?" I ask, irritated I let myself trust him as much as I have.

"I wouldn't be able to think up a new topping if you paid me a million dollars. I guess just every time you talk about what is going to go into this it surprises me more. And what does a little savory, a little sweet mean?" he asks, and my irritation melts away as I laugh.

"Hey," he says, his voice edged like mine was a minute ago.

I wave a flour dusted hand in wait gesture as I try to control my giggles before he gets too hurt.

"Sorry," I say. "Sometimes I forget most people haven't grown up around restaurants their whole life. I just realized how immersed I am." I take some more breaths while his face softens out and he goes back to looking like he's listening and interested in what I'm saying again, now that he knows I was laughing at myself.

"There are essentially two kinds of taste buds, savory is anything that hits the salt category, meats, etcetera. Sweet is anything that hits the sugar taste buds. So, what most recipes are trying to do is find the balance between those and have different flavors that play off each other well. Pizza is popular, in part, because most of the sweet is in the tomato sauce, so you can load up on the savory. People don't realize that's why it hits so good on the taste quotient," I say, rambling on about the very food I complain about regularly, singing its praises on reflex.

"Huh, I had no idea." He gets a far away look on his face and one side of his mouth turns up before he says, "Is that why most people don't like Hawaiian?" I laugh and point at him.

"Exactly," I say.

"Too much sweet," we say at the same time.

Somehow, although my feet feel like they're going to fall off and I want to pass out, I make it to five o'clock and hand the reigns off to Junior and my dad who makes an unusual appearance for the closing shift.

At least I know Junior won't be unsupervised for the busiest night of the week. Maybe they got my text. I'm smiling to myself about how much I hope they all got the message and Mom sat them both down for a chat while I take off my apron when Campbell comes up next to me.

"Do you," he starts and swallows, taking a long pause while he takes off his own apron before he speaks again, "do you want to go somewhere with me tonight?"

What I want is to go to sleep, but my stomach takes that chance to growl so loud I think half the customers heard it, reminding me I never did sit down and eat after my meager bowl of cereal.

"Okay, but can this somewhere involve food?" I ask and smile as he grins and holds out his arm for me to link mine into.

"I thought you would never ask," he says, and we grab coats and head out the back door.

The evening is crisp and clear, if it remains this way it will be the perfect night to stare at the stars that manage to shine through the lights of the city.

"So, tonight, I'm taking the next step in fake dating," he says, walking me to what I now know is his aunt's car.

"You drove?" I ask, grinning.

"Yes," he says, slow and careful like he's not sure about the tone of my voice.

"When you left your house this morning you had this plan, didn't you?" I ask, and he laughs.

"Get in," he says, climbing into the driver's side and I climb in on the passenger side.

"If you must know, yes I had this planned, but you looked wiped out most of the day so I was starting to doubt you would say yes." He starts the car and maneuvers us out of the parking lot.

"This grand plan of yours, what does it entail this time? I am tired, so I'm not sure I'm up for more karaoke," I say, leaning back into the seat and closing my eyes for a minute while he laughs.

"Come on, karaoke was great."

"Not the point, but yes."

"Omar has the same crowd from last time over to our house tonight for some big tournament and I thought it would be fun to hang out with them again. It fits into your whole mission."

"I get to see your house?" I sit up and open my eyes, my stomach dancing and my nerves making my cheeks heat up. Being inside Omar's house was not part of what I thought fake dating would entail.

"Yep, and my aunt will try and feed you so much you'll gain fifty pounds in a single evening," he says and laughs.

"Deacon asked me to bring snacks from the restaurant next time we all get together for karaoke," I say, taking deep breaths and focusing on how good the last time went so my hands don't start shaking.

"Tonight, if we bring snacks my aunt will take it personally, like we don't like her food. Trust me when I say Deacon will have more than enough." He puts his hand on mine, a reassurance that actually helps.

His ability to calm my nerves means my cheeks stop flaming and my hands no longer want to shake.

To turn into the driveway of a blue, two story, fourplex, he takes his hand off of mine and we wedge past two cars to park in what looks like it used to be the front yard, but is now gravel. The front yard is relegated to a strip of green and then a border of flower beds that are filled with the kind of scaffolding I associate with pictures of gardens with vines growing up them. Now they're bare and all the beds look lonely without any green.

"Do you all grow fruits and vegetables?" I ask as we unbuckle, and he turns off the car.

"No, just my aunt. Everyone gives all the beds over to my aunt for her to do with as she pleases, they get fresh stuff out of it half the year and don't have to do the work." We climb out of the car and I think about the tiny backyard we have at home, smaller than my bedroom, and how we have never, not once, tried to grow anything other than grass.

Maybe I should get a plant for my room, our house is as lonely of green as the beds are in winter.

We walk up to the door of the last townhouse and before Campbell reaches for the door knob I hear the muffled bass tones of Deacon's voice asking for more food. It makes me smile as Campbell opens the door and we're hit with a fantastic smell of spices. So many spices.

"They're here," Katie calls, and runs from the kitchen island everyone is crowded around to hug me.

I squeeze her back, but my brain is stopped. People never hug me that are just friends. It is so foreign, and I thought it was something that only happened on TV shows.

"You have no idea how glad I am you're here, I just want to watch them play and laugh at them. You're not planning on playing, are you?" She rattles out as she pulls me toward the kitchen.

"Let her breathe, Katie," Omar says, and laughs when she sticks her tongue out at him.

"At least let her hold her boyfriend's hand. Are you trying to make a move?" Deacon asks, pointing at Katie with what looks like a french fry.

"Oh, Deacon the pure of heart, look at you watching out for your man over here," Katie says, laughing as she lets go of me to dig into the spread herself.

Before us on the island are so many different foods a whole restaurant could be based off of them. I grab a French fry first, and it isn't a potato, instead I find some flaky fried and seasoned yucca in my mouth. A noise of contentment makes its way out of my mouth.

"Ah, I knew a girl who lives above a pizza shop would appreciate all of this," Deacon says with a wink.

"I've never had yucca prepared like this, it's delicious," I say, grabbing another and popping it into my mouth.

"Why thank you," a woman says as she places a plate of empanadas among the other delights we're all grabbing from, with greed in our eyes.

"Mom, this is Olivia, the one I told you about," Omar says, gesturing to me.

The fact his mother has heard of me makes me blush and avert my gaze.

"Olivia, this is my mom, Carmen," Omar says.

"It's nice to meet you, and this is really wonderful food," I say, looking back at Carmen who gives me a small smile, her dark eyes shrewd as she takes me in.

"Very nice to meet you, too," she says, her v sounding like a b and her accent more pronounced than Campbell's, or Omar who doesn't have one at all.

"So, you are dating my nephew, and you just met him," she says, and I choke on my fry.

"Tia, please," Campbell says, placing his hand on the small of my back as if to support me.

The gesture doesn't stop my cheeks from heating up, or from the heat growing into my hairline. My whole face is hotter than the sun by the time Carmen raises an eyebrow and turns and walks away.

I let out the breath I was holding in a whoosh and Deacon laughs.

"What's so funny, Deacon?" I ask, shooting him a look because it's messed up he enjoys my humiliation so much.

"Nothing," he says, holding his hands in the surrender pose and I look to Campbell and Omar for some hint of what the hell is so funny.

"Don't worry about it, she's just being protective," Campbell says to me, but he's looking at Omar with a hint in his eyes that something is definitely going on.

"They don't want to tell you that it's because you're white. Keep complimenting her cooking. Aunties love for you to eat a ton and ask for more. Trust me," Katie says, her grin devious as she loads a plate up with more food than I normally eat in a day and hands it to me.

"Katie, you're white," I say, taking it from her and Deacon almost falls out of his chair laughing.

"She has a black dad," Theresa says, laughing.

"Oh, I…" I am so stupid. I cringe and look to see Katie trying to stifle a laugh. It just confuses me, and with my face on fire I wring my hands together to stop their shaking. This is it. The moment I blunder into losing all my new friends because I didn't know and I had to open my stupid, stupid mouth and now I've not only burnt my chance to a crisp, but I probably insulted Katie somehow.

"Look, Deacon, she's even more pure than you," Katie says, elbowing Deacon, who plants a meaty hand on my shoulder.

"One of her dad's is my uncle, we get it. You didn't know, although it is absolutely the cutest thing I've ever seen that you're about to have a panic attack about pointing out the obvious," Deacon says, and Katie elbows him again, this time hard, in the gut.

"My dads call me a very, very pale half black," Katie says and smiles her wait for it smile. "Deacon is going to hear all about it from our Auntie Deb, and I still want us to sit together while these fools lose and bitch about it."

"Hey, hey, hey. You don't need to be telling Auntie Deb anything," Deacon says and grabs at Katie's hand as she dances around him to my other side, cackling.

"Why do I have the feeling he's in deep shit?" I ask.

She doesn't answer, just grabs my heaping plate of food and drags me away from everyone, Deacon groaning behind us.

CHAPTER 15

Katie leads me down a set of stairs and into a basement that hasn't been redecorated since long before I was born. There's wood paneling on the walls, mustardy yellow shag carpeting, and patterned brown couches set up around a green pool table. It's the ugliest room I've ever seen.

"Ignore the décor. Carmen says she won't redecorate until after Omar moves out because he and his friends would destroy anything nice she put down here. She means us, we're the destroyers," Katie says, plopping onto one of the couches.

"Well, she's not entirely wrong," I say, sitting next to her while she laughs and the others barrel down the stairs, their footsteps as loud as the roar of the restaurant on a Saturday night like tonight. The noise makes me feel more comfortable.

"So, what exactly is going on?" I ask, as Campbell sits on my other side and loops his arm around my back, pulling me back into the couch cushions.

"They are all going to play a tournament of pool, we are

going to watch and laugh at how bad they are," Campbell says, with a smile.

"Why don't you play?" I ask, although I have no idea why any of them are playing this game, or why it would be fun for us to watch. I've played pool exactly once, and it was a disaster.

"Campbell isn't allowed to play," Omar says from where he's racking the balls at the end of the table.

"Not allowed? What did he do? Break a cue?" I ask.

"Worse," Theresa says, chalking up her own cue.

Campbell is pointedly not looking at me and his hand is now just resting along my side instead of holding me.

"Alright, she's never seen it. We've got to let him do the thing," Jenna, another cheerleader says. "It's too impressive for his girl not to experience it."

"This is an experience thing?" I ask, and Campbell takes a deep breath.

"Okay, Olivia, come on. I'm not sure I can do it, but I'll try," he says, taking my hand and pulling me to my feet.

We move to the pool table where the balls are in their triangle shape at one end and the cue ball is at the other. Deacon hands me a cue which may as well be a goat for all I know to do with it.

"Here," Campbell says, his voice low and hushed. He maneuvers me to standing, bent over the pool table, my fingers barely touching the cue, his hands intertwined with mine and his front laying against my back.

"Close your eyes."

I do as I'm told, it helps slow my hammering heart and cool the heat growing in my cheeks.

"Breathe in," he says, and I feel him take a breath with me. "Breathe out."

As we breathe out together he moves our hands a fraction, the cue smacking into the cue ball and a resounding crack and smaller knocks sound as he pulls our hands and the cue up and out of the way of the balls flying across the surface of the table. My eyes are wide open, and I stare, dumbfounded, as three of the balls find their way to a pocket.

"No way," I whisper.

He doesn't answer me. He just moves with me around the table, taking shot after shot, sinking them all with his hands in mine the whole time and no one, not one of our friends, saying a word.

When the table is completely clear, every single ball sunk into a pocket, he steps back, leaving me holding the cue.

"That's why he isn't allowed to play. He's a shark," Omar says, his voice hushed, sounding reverent.

But I barely hear him, I'm staring at Campbell as he retrieves all the sunk balls and reracks them for the next people to play. Those long, thin fingers moving so deftly around the pool table it's clear, as if it wasn't already, that this is a major part of his world. One he didn't even mention to me.

His face is blank, the life in it, is dimmed somehow by this game they've made him play. By this show we've just put on.

In silence I hand the cue to Theresa and go back to sit by Katie on the couch. She hands me one of the empanadas from the massive pile of food I haven't eaten yet.

The flavors explode in my mouth, my stomach growls in pleasure as Campbell sits next to me and pulls me back into the cushions again, his half smile back on his face.

"I'm glad you like those, they're my favorite. Nothing like empanadas to get you through the bad stuff," he says, quiet near my ear.

His voice quavers at bad stuff, and it makes me think his comment means something specific. In the middle of this group, I don't want to ask him what that is. Instead I look at him, our faces inches apart, and try to tell him with my eyes that whatever the bad is, this is good. Whatever lessened that light in his face, it doesn't have to anymore.

My face must say more than I realize because he smiles and squeezes me, taking the empanada out of my hand and stealing a bite.

"Hey," I say.

Katie laughs and I take back my food. The rest of the group start their tournament, their skills far less impressive now that I know what Campbell can do. We chat and I eat, the pressure off of me to be entertaining and instead I just get to be entertained.

Theresa and Deacon are good, Omar is competent, but Jenna… she squeaks "oh, shit," so reliably after every wayward shot she takes, that about the fourth time she shoots all of us say it at the same time she does.

Hours later, the food is gone, Theresa has won the tournament, and everyone is departing for the night.

Campbell and I are the first to leave, because he says he has to drive me home.

"I'm so glad you were here," Katie says as she hugs me goodbye.

"Yeah, me too," I say. And it isn't just that Omar has been attentive all night and this fake dating seems to be working. Or that Campbell is turning into a wonderful friend, along with Katie and Deacon. It's that this place, this foray into someone else's life, is making me feel like I have one of my own.

Omar gives me a hug after Katie, holding on for a beat too long, and he smiles at me as he pulls away before Campbell touches me on the back and we turn to go.

"Well," Campbell says, and clears his throat, "I think it's working." He walks to the driver's side of the car and I get in on my side.

Once we're inside the car and moving out of the driveway I get up the nerve to say anything. Tonight feels heavy in some ways, and I don't want to step wrong while the weight is on my back.

"Thank you for this. Although I think your aunt might hate me," I say, smiling to lighten the mood and turn the conversation to the things I feel equipped to handle.

"My aunt is usually not like that. I'm sure she doesn't hate you," he says, navigating the traffic.

"Is she like that with Omar's dates?"

"Maybe. I haven't been around for any of his dates being brought home."

Omar hasn't dated anyone in the month or so since Campbell came to town, I would know, the whole school would be talking about it if he had. I breathe out a nervous breath, it's probably how she reacts to anyone dating one of her boys, and that's how I was introduced. So, it's no big deal, except what will she think when Campbell and I stop our fake dating?

"What you're telling me is, I need to win over your aunt as much as I do your cousin, so she doesn't kill me if this crazy idea of yours actually works." I laugh as he cocks his head and opens and closes his mouth.

"You didn't think of that, huh?" I ask, and drop my head back onto the headrest. This officially just blew up in my face.

"In my defense, I didn't realize she would act all protective beyond making sure people in general don't be awful to me. But now I think we have some work to do," he says, smiling that puckish smile and quirking an eyebrow.

"Uh oh, that seems ominous," I say, more willing to play along with whatever devious plan he has in mind because his first one managed to score me friends.

"Not ominous, brilliant," he says, tapping his temple.

CHAPTER 16

*H*aving nothing to do but wait for the saffron to come from Campbell's sources for me to start test cooking, I get to sleep in on Sunday, enjoy my shrunken schedule all week, and sleep until the regular morning prep on Saturday after closing Friday night staying up later than I have all week. No more wee hours cleaning after close, only to wake too early trying to work on my pizza. No more closing every night to get up and go to school in the morning. It's glorious.

When Campbell walks into the kitchen on Saturday morning, I'm humming the tune to the song he had me sing at karaoke.

"Good morning. I told you that song was good," he says, smiling and getting his apron on.

"Yes, you did," I say, smiling at him and focusing back on the dough in my hands.

He starts prepping the chop, gathering the items he needs and it's hard not to watch him, to pay attention to what I need to do. He moves with an ease and efficiency that suggests he's worked here longer than he actually has. He's already found his rhythm. It makes me smile.

"So," he says, and peeks up from what he's doing to smile at me. "What are you doing tonight?"

I laugh, and so does he. This fake dating thing is turning out to be fun.

"No plans," I say, trying to not screw up the dough I'm working on as I get more distracted by trying in vain to think up whatever crazy thing he'll plan for us to do next. "What do you have in mind?"

"Ah, well," he says, and leans toward me as if it's a secret. "You're coming to my place tonight so operation make Aunt Carmen fall madly in love with you can commence."

"Wait, really?" I ask, stopping what I'm doing entirely to stare at him. My heart starts to pound harder, this could be more important for me to be successful at than any of his other crazy ideas.

"Yep, but don't worry. This, I think, will be your favorite," he says and winks at me.

I smile and return my attention to what I have to get done before we open. Campbell and I make a good team, we get done with enough time to sit and have a drink while we wait.

"This paella pizza, tell me what the plan is; how are you going to make that happen?" he asks.

"So, you know the saffron threads will be worked into the dough, that's the easiest part," I say, my hands getting animated as my excitement grows. "The next bit is going to be the sauce, how to strike the proper balance of spices to make sure I get that proper paella flavor. I have some paella recipes of my mom's I'm going to draw off of as a start and then it's just flavoring to taste and writing it all down as I do. The really tricky part is the topping. I don't think I'll do cheese at all, but I need to find a way to fry up some clams and calamari thin enough that they don't get soggy and thick enough that they don't get dried out from the double cooking, frying and then baking when it's all together."

"Why do you have to bake it all together? Can't you bake the crust and then add the sauce and the toppings to an already done crust?" he asks.

"I mean…" I say, thinking about it. "I suppose. But, part of the joy of pizza is the idea that all these separate things come together and become greater than each thing on its own. It feels wrong to not try to get all the flavors floating through the oven and seeping into each other."

He quirks an eyebrow and the smile he gets is one for an especially adorable puppy.

Not sure I like his response, I furrow my brow the question about to pop out of my mouth.

"You just waxed philosophical about pizza."

And I'm laughing, dropping my face into my hands and barely able to stay upright, laughing.

"Oh, my god. I'm pathetic. Who talks like that? About pizza?" I ask, cracking up.

"It isn't pathetic, it's cute as hell, and if your parents heard you talk like that, they would never think even giving Junior an option to take over the business was a good idea," he says.

I don't have time to ponder my parent's wisdom, or lack thereof, before Nelson and Gina arrive and start getting ready for the lunch rush.

CHAPTER 17

Campbell and I make our way to his aunt's car through the rain after our shift is over.

Shutting the door behind me, wiping my wet hair out of my eyes I take a deep breath of the fresh fall downpour smell. I love the different smells of the rain. People in Seattle sometimes struggle with Seasonal Affective Disorder because there are so many grey or rainy days, not me. There is nothing more refreshing than the newness of all the different smells of the rain.

In the summer, a rain smells like a cool drink when you're parched. Like dust is being rinsed off the world.

A spring rain smells like growth and rebirth, all the new of the world coming out to say hello.

This rain, a cool fall rain, smells of school and football and all the kinds of traditions that start this time of year and carry us through the cold of winter.

When the rains come in winter, it's usually a respite from the cold days and they smell of wood smoke from the chimneys in houses, and hot cocoa, and fuzzy blankets.

Campbell maneuvers the car out of the lot, the rhythmic swishing of the car's wipers lulling this moment into one of greater beauty. Just sitting in a car, with rain coming down, next to a friend. It isn't an experience I have often.

"So, what are we doing tonight?" I ask, looking over at him. The light coming through the wavery outside is turning him into a soft focus picture.

"Nope, no hints. I want to surprise you. You'll like it, I promise. So just sit tight, we're almost there," He says, reaching over to squeeze my hand.

I'm not nervous right now, he's working his calming magic on me again, but he's still reaching out to try and settle any concerns I may have. It makes me squeeze his hand back, which brings a soft smile to his face.

Pulling into the driveway of his house, there is one less car than there was before, but he still parks in the gravel area.

We dart through the rain to the front door, Campbell opening it to let me in.

Inside, his aunt is in the kitchen and seeing her sends a jolt down my spine and makes my cheeks heat up. I'm not sure she wants me to be here.

She smiles at us, her careful, guarded, and regarding smile I recognize as the same one she wore before.

"Hi, Tia," Campbell says, taking off his sodden jacket and taking mine from me to hang on hooks by the front door.

"Campbell, Olivia, come in here and let's get started," she says, nodding our way.

I swallow and look to Campbell, he puts his hand on the small of my back and smiles, telling me it's okay. I take a deep breath and go to the kitchen and his aunt, waiting.

On the countertop are bowls, yucca in a bowl of water, and graters. What are we doing here?

"Campbell and Omar tell me your family has a restaurant," she says, placing three cutting boards on the counter.

"Yes, we own Joe's, the pizzeria," I say, following Campbell's lead to wash my hands in the sink, up to the elbow, the same way we do at work.

"Ah, pizza. Well, today my nephew has told me you would like to learn how I make my yucca," she says, her eyebrow quirked at Campbell.

"That's why we're here?" I ask, almost jumping up and down. "Yes, please. Your fries and empanadas were amazing."

"Thank you." She smiles at me, gone is the careful aspect of it. The way to this woman's heart is through her own cooking.

"So, what we do first is soak them for a long time. Which I have already done. Now we are going to grate them. Very, very fine grate."

We get to work, all of us side by side as she tells me this method allows her to use the yucca as almost an all purpose dough. It still requires frying, but the way she does it means we can roll it out like a pie crust, it holds together, and is never too tough.

We laugh at her stories, I tell many of my own, including trusting her with my idea for the pizza competition. She suggests spices I had not thought to use for the sauce, and my brain goes flying through the possibility of using her yucca technique to make the fries a side at the restaurant. I will call them Carmen fries.

She is a genius, and by the time Campbell and I are saying goodbye, she is giving me a hug, tucking my hair behind my ear and loading my arms full of wrapped up Carmen fries and empanadas.

"Thank you so much, this was amazing," I say, for the hundredth time tonight.

"You're very welcome, *linda*," she says.

Her smile is so wide I blush and lose my nerve to ask what *linda* means.

Campbell and I make our way out to the car, the sky is dark and cloudy, but for the moment free of rain.

As he's driving me home, the heat of my food packages seeping into my lap, I ask, "What does *linda* mean?"

"In the Dominican, it means beautiful."

CHAPTER 18

The following Saturday, Campbell comes in in the morning at a run. He isn't late, so I stop with my hands in the dough and watch as he darts past the aprons entirely and comes to stand before me, a package in his hand, and his face wearing a massive grin.

"Ask me," he says, almost bouncing.

"Uh, what's up, Campbell?" I ask, not able to repress grinning.

"It came." His voice is quiet and conspiratorial.

I don't get it. Whatever has him so beyond excited, for a second, I don't understand. And then my brain kicks in, my saffron. The package we've been waiting on from the Dominican is what he must be holding.

I squeal, my arms flying from the dough to fling flour all over the place.

"Oh, no." I dart to the sink to wash off my hands as he laughs behind me.

"So, what are you doing tomorrow morning?" he asks.

"We are going to be working on that pizza dough," I say, giving him a hug. "Thank you so much."

"All I did was ask my mom to send me some spices. She was happy to for the girl that gave me job," he says, hugging me back, the box resting against my back where he's holding on to it.

I pull away and he hands me the box, a huge grin on his face that matches the one I know I'm wearing. The aroma of saffron is spilling through it, but for now, I just hide it in the back of the pantry behind some flour.

"We don't have time to play with it right now, although I'm dying to. If we open it, I think the smell would let even Junior know something is up," I say, leaving the pantry to rejoin a now apron wearing Campbell on the prep.

"So, when do you get the other ingredients you need? Should we go to Pike Place tonight?" he asks.

"It would be best to go to the market the morning we're going to cook them. I don't think I'll have time tomorrow. This whole sneaking around with only so much time for it is a problem," I say, chewing my lip, trying to think around the schedule of the restaurant and when Junior and Dad are likely to be around.

"Okay, so send me," Campbell says.

"That's nice of you, but I feel like I need to pick all the ingredients myself," I say, and the grin falls from his face.

"You've already helped so much getting me the saffron and I have to do this to prove to my parents I can," I say, rushing to get the words out, to make him understand, it isn't a slight on him.

"It's okay, Olivia. I get it," he says, looking only at his work in front of him.

But he doesn't get it, I can tell. I don't know how to change it, to let him know I need to prove this to myself as much as to them.

I keep my mouth shut, doing the rest of the prep for the day in silence with mounting frustration. This is my chance to work for my future, I need to stake that claim, climb that mountaintop, as much on my own as possible.

Of course, he got me the saffron, but I could have gotten it on my own, he was my source for it, but this is still my project.

Does he think this is somehow about him?

My brother thinks everything is about him; I didn't expect it of Campbell. Stupid me.

The rest of my shift is spent running through my entire friendship with Campbell in the back of my mind, questioning his motives for all the kindnesses and willingness to help me.

He's been just trying to pay me back for giving him a job, I decide. He needs to know he doesn't have to continue to do things for me out of obligation. He comes to work, he gets paid. That's our mutual obligation. If we are going to be true friends, he needs to break away from this sense of duty centered around this place. We need to be friends separate from this restaurant.

As we're both wrapping up our jobs for the night, I get the courage to actually talk to him about it.

"Hey, Olivia, can I talk to you for a minute?" Dad asks from behind me as I'm about to open my mouth and speak to Campbell, who heads out the back door.

"Yeah, Dad," I say and head to the office.

I sit in the seat across the desk from him, he no longer looks comfortable behind the desk, and I sure don't feel comfortable on this side.

"Listen, I know Mom said you needed to step back and find balance, and I know your text message was needed because we can't let those things get out of hand, but I don't want you sending anymore messages to Mom. Please just send them to me," he says, his head lowered and no animation on his face.

"You look tired, Dad," I say.

"I'm exhausted, that's the point, damn it," he says, his face reddening and his eyes boring into me. All his exhaustion of the minutes before is gone.

"What are you talking about? And don't yell at me," I say, my cheeks on fire and angry tears building in my eyes.

"I… I'm sorry, Livvy," he says, and takes a deep breath, closing his eyes for a second longer than necessary.

"The issue is your mother insists on trying to do everything, and I can't let her put that stress on herself. She needs to only focus on getting better. I'm trying to get Junior up to speed too, but he doesn't have the experience you do yet. Can you just, please, help me with this for a little while," he says, his hands gripping each other in front of him on the desktop.

"Don't tell Mom anything, and just take care of the problems as they pop up? Or," I say, and the desperate, building need to angry cry is gone, but a tear falls anyway, "are there specific things you want me to start doing again? Like closing every night and all the ordering and paperwork?"

"Yes, I'm sorry, but I need you to start doing a lot of that again. I can't take care of your Mom and do all of it at the same time; she shouldn't be doing any of it, and until Junior can pick it up, I need you. Please."

The please kills me. The fact that I know what it's like now to occasionally get to spend time with friends, to sleep, to be able to work on things I need to do for me without constantly trying to fit all of my work in around school, makes going back to having work be my whole life again more painful.

It was only a matter of time. I think I always knew it, but the look on my dad's face makes it much more obvious.

"Okay, Dad." There is nothing else I can say. Not when I

know he's right that Mom needs to be able to focus on getting better, and he needs to spend time taking care of her so she can.

"Thanks, Livvy. I love you; we'll get through this," he says, standing from behind the desk to pat my shoulder as he leaves the office.

CHAPTER 19

There aren't enough hours in the day, and I've been living on borrowed ones. I walk out of the office after Dad's little chat and check that he's on the floor along with Junior for the closing shift.

After everything he said, I was half sure I would need to close tonight. Instead I take off my apron and go upstairs.

Mom is asleep on the couch with the television on. I tuck her blanket tighter around her feet because the nerve damage in them makes it harder for her to keep them warm.

I wander down the hall to my room. The poster for the competition is on the wall by my desk. Dad never assured me Junior wouldn't be taking over, that my hard work wouldn't just end with him destroying it all anyway. I take down the poster and drop it into the trash can by my desk.

All in one day, I get a great step forward on my plan to win the competition, only for my dad to make it impossible for me to be able to have time to work on it, and my friendship with Campbell becomes questionable.

Mondays don't suck, I decide, Saturdays do.

I grab my phone from the desktop and throw myself onto my bed.

Dad just informed me I am going to be closing every weeknight and doing the paperwork again so he can take care of Mom. He said nothing about me taking over. I don't think I'll be doing the contest. I appreciate all your help. Of course, I still paid you back, it's rubber banded amongst your tips tonight, so look in your envelope.

The text to Campbell sits with the curser to type more blinking at me while I decide whether or not to type the rest of the message I want to send. I bite my lip and feel the anger building in me, the waviness of my vision increasing. I don't want to cry anymore tonight.

Don't worry about an early morning tomorrow, I'll be getting in at seven for the prep.

I send my text to Campbell and focus on the pile of boxes in the corner of my room I didn't notice when I walked in.

My new room décor has arrived. Yay.

Rolling over, I bury my face in my pillows and decide five o'clock isn't too early to go to sleep. But my phone dings telling me I have a text.

One of the last things I feel like doing is looking at a text. If it's Dad asking me to come back downstairs to work, I don't want to know. Looking at my phone tells me its Campbell. So, I click the button to see what he has to say.

Are you shitting me? Don't give up now. I'll be there at 4 so we can get everything done.

He was so obviously upset earlier, and now he wants to help. I must have read him wrong. The fact he wants to help still bouys my spirits, I have to find the time between not closing Saturdays and opening Sundays to work on the competition. It isn't much, but I can do it. And getting the paperwork done is going to mean at least an hour every shift in the office.

Thank you.

I text back to Campbell and look on my phone at the staffing schedule. Making notations in my personal calendar of the times Junior isn't on shift with me so I can step away and get the office work done. I don't trust him out there by himself.

Dad and Junior are both scheduled every week day during the day, Nelson and Andrew are doing all those prep days so Dad and Junior aren't showing up until ten when we open and Mom can have Dad take her to her appointments in the mornings. But at least some of those days she's going to have a hard time and he's going to be pulled away. What we need is another manager. Someone to at least do the ordering, but half the suppliers want payment right away and my family are the only ones who are signers on the account.

I'm going to have to devise a cash system for paying suppliers. Dad will hate it; he doesn't like having that much cash on hand; it makes him nervous we'll be robbed or the money itself will get us all sick. He never thought about how dirty money is until the virus, now he's paranoid but won't go away from using it because he says it's elitist to have just cards. I can figure a way around all of it, a way to have another set of hands help us though this.

CHAPTER 20

Three o'clock in the morning comes too soon, even when sleep came by seven the night before. My body doesn't want to get up; it feels unnatural. I do it, though, swinging my legs down to the floor because I'm excited about today. Today is the first test of my idea.

My shower wakes me up, but it's the sugary cereal to the real rescue, giving me enough energy to get dressed and start tearing into the boxes of my new décor.

Rug boxes are easy to tell from the boxes holding anything else. I roll up my old rug and shove it in the corner. My new one wants to stay rolled at the end, but I tuck the side under the posts of my bed and stand back to take it in.

Cream with sepia geometric shapes in a stripe, simple, and I like it. It brightens my room and makes it look a little more like a chic loft somewhere, a modern touch among all the antique aesthetics of my turret.

Next is my bedding, I don't wad it up and shove it in the corner, but I do lug it through the house and dump it in the laundry room. I'll wash it and put it in the linen closet later.

For now, I grab fresh sheets from the linen closet, because a whole fresh bed sounds like a perfect way to end what I am determined to be good day.

Making my bed lets me try and prepare different crusts in my mind, when in the process is it best to add the saffron? I'll have to try at least one that is just a dusting on top of the dough while it's wet like I do with garlic for the regular pizza. I also want to do some with the saffron inside the dough, before I throw it.

My new bedding has three extra pillows in addition to the two that go with my sheets and the two shams. I don't know what the point is to so many pillows, by the time I'm done trying to artfully place them on my bed, half of the whole bed seems like it's pillow.

I stand back to look at the very different bed I have now. It's beautiful. The bedding is a simple quilted look with tiny ruffles acting like stripes, in a copper color, complete with some threads that must be metallic in some way because they almost sparkle in the lamplight.

Bedding and a new rug is all I needed. The room feels infinitely more me now. And I haven't even gotten my desk yet.

With a decided spring in my step, I drag the empty boxes through my house and down the steps to the recycle bin behind the restaurant.

"Olivia?" I hear behind me and jump a foot as I twirl around.

Campbell stands not far behind me, bags in his hands, in the light from the back door of the restaurant. It's shining on his head so that he looks like he got highlights in his deep brown hair.

"You scared the shit out of me," I say, trying to slow my speeding heart rate.

He chuckles and I smile, still tentative because we haven't really worked anything out, and I don't know how to start.

"Aunt Carmen sent breakfast," he says, holding up the bag in his hands.

"Bless that woman. Come inside," I say, wrapping my arms around myself and trying not to shiver.

"So, what is the first thing we need to do?" he asks once we're inside with the door shut on the chill dark of early morning.

"First, dish the food up; we have plenty of plates," I gesture to the wall of shelves with the dishes on them. "I'm going to run back up stairs and grab my notebook."

I dart up the stairs on my toes, trying to avoid a clatter that will wake up my family.

My notebook rests on my desk, and I take a second to admire the new look of my room before I make my way down to the restaurant again.

Campbell is getting forks, setting them next to plates on one of the prep islands, but I go into the pantry and retrieve my hidden box of saffron before I go to sit across from him.

My notebook opens to my list of terrible topping ideas, I thumb through until I get to the page with my scribbles detailing the various ways I could include the saffron in a crust and turn it toward Campbell.

The empanada makes me warm from the inside out, all the remaining chill from outside chased far away by the flavors, the spices, and the love I know Carmen cooks into each one. By the time I'm done eating, my body has also shaken off the last vestiges of sleep and I'm more than ready to get started.

"So we can get these all started and just add saffron threads to two of them, right?" Campbell says around a bite of empanada. He won't look at me, instead focusing on the notebook.

"Yeah, I'll get it all out." It's easier to deal with his lack of eye contact, and the remnants of our conversation yesterday that I still can't completely deal with right now, if I'm just getting tucked into some dough.

The first step is to proof the yeast, so I follow the usual balance of warm water, sugar, and yeast and mix it all up, only then do I mix in some saffron threads and set it aside. Two doughs get that treatment and the last just the basic yeast proofing, set down on the other side of the ovens from the first two so I don't screw them all up.

We wait seven minutes while we each grind some of the saffron threads in mortar and pestles. When the timer goes off, we mix our yeast starters with flour and salt.

"Do you think I should brush some sofrito on top of the dough separate from the tomato sauce? I was planning on just cooking it into the tomato sauce," I say, thinking out loud to Campbell.

"Um," Campbell says, mixing the dough he's in charge of, "I don't see how it could hurt. Although I didn't even think about how that might change the flavor. Why not try it both ways?"

I don't say it out loud, but I have to think about all of it. About how this needs to be done right, or I won't win. And after the conversation with Dad, I am more certain now than I have ever been that I need to win and take over this place.

"Are you sure you don't want to try a version with some cheese? I don't think mozzarella would ruin it, and it would embrace the traditional idea of pizza a little more," he says, apparently now onto my trend of second and third guessing.

"You're right, I should at least try it," I say. "Let's get this dough thrown, I want this one to go in as is, but those two need to get dusted."

I throw all three doughs and put them on the paddles, Campbell follows behind me and dusts the crushed up saffron on two of them. He also slides them all into the ovens.

"Okay. I'll hide this, and then we can get the prep done," I say, realizing we'll have an hour and a half extra with nothing to do.

"Should I try making the sauce?" I ask, spinning abruptly back toward Campbell and catch him staring after me. It's the first time we've held eye contact since he came inside.

He looks at the clock, seeing the same thing I do, and takes a deep breath.

"Why not?" he asks, but his voice is careful, like he isn't committing to his words.

"I think Dad has some seafood stock left over from a soup he made for Mom. I'll go upstairs and grab it." I put the saffron away in the pantry and make my way up the stairs, followed by the tendrils of aroma coming out of the ovens.

Our fridge is always a strange place, some combination of leftovers, ingredients, and dishes partly made, always labeled. Lately it has also included a lot of half gone soups and smoothies, evidence of Dad's constant search for more foods Mom can keep down.

The seafood stock is clearly labeled; it won't be missed. Dad made Mom soup out of it yesterday and she didn't get two bites in before she asked for a smoothie instead.

I have no guilt about grabbing the Tupperware and heading back down to the restaurant, but something slows my feet on the way down the stairs. Eventually, Campbell and I will have to figure this all out, I deserve to know why he got so upset with me. But I don't have the emotional bandwidth to deal with it right now.

"Alright, I got it," I say, coming into the kitchen to find Campbell chopping up peppers and a collection of all the ingredients we will need for the sofrito arrayed next to him on the counter.

"Oh, um, thank you." There is little I feel like I can say. He's being kind and I shouldn't push that away with all of the questions rolling around in the back of my brain.

I get the stock heating and get to my own mincing and fine chopping, both of us adding to the pan as we get our ingredients ready. Meanwhile, I start a pot of our house tomato sauce heating, separating part of both into a third pot to mix them together.

"Why don't we split each of the doughs and dip them into the sauces for flavor testing?" Campbell asks and his voice makes me jump.

The tension I feel being near him was becoming background noise while I poured myself into cooking and the familiar movements, but with his voice, the tension in me snaps taught again.

"That," I choke a little on my own words, trying to get them out of my mouth and not let the heat building up my neck flood my face with a blush, "that's a good idea."

"I have to admit I find it weird that you do all this in separate pieces and not just make a bunch of whole pizzas and go with the one that tastes the best," he says, washing up his area and putting things away now that he's done.

Stirring the sauces gives me an excuse not to answer for a minute, to try and explain what it is that made me go with this strategy, because it was instinctual, not thought out.

"Well, I could have done that. But by doing it this way, I can make notes of what each piece and item brings to the table separately and then when they are combined I can hopefully pinpoint what, if anything, goes wrong with the flavoring." The sauces need to sit, so I have to physically step back from the pots to avoid over stirring them, but I adjust the heat on the burners to what each needs.

My notebook still rests next to where we ate and I start making notes in it of everything we've done, the new ideas I've had, exactly how much of each ingredient went into each item.

Campbell doesn't say a word, the silence grows heavy and yet he still doesn't speak.

The timer for the crusts goes off, he and I pull them all from the ovens, their smell mixing with the sauces and creating a brew in the air that makes me hungry, even though we just ate.

We go back to cleaning things up, and even get started on some of the prep to open before I grab off a chunk of one of the crusts and dip it into the seafood sofrito and take a bite.

"Meh," I say, and put the chunk of crust down.

"Meh? How can any of these be meh?" he asks, but follows my lead. When he pops the bite into his mouth he smiles.

"What?" I ask, doing the same again with a piece of different crust, which is better, and I note it in my book. "Why are you smiling?" I ask, over my shoulder.

"That bite was one of the best bites of food I've had in a long time and you just dismissed it," he says, shaking his head. "Perfectionist."

"Taste the others and then tell me that. You'll see, I'm right." I go through the tasting process of a piece of each crust dipped in each sauce and makes notes of every flavor combination along the way, the ones that work and the ones that don't.

"Wow, okay, I never thought I would say this, but pizza can really be anything. This makes me think of paella right away and you're not even done. The best one is the saffron in the dough with the mixed sauce," he says, washing his hands after he pops another piece of his chosen combination into his mouth.

I write his vote down in my notebook but write next to it why he's wrong. With the addition of the toppings, especially the smooth, calming taste of the mozzarella, I think I need to use the crust with saffron in the dough and sprinkled on top with the mixed sauce.

CHAPTER 21

The following Saturday morning, Campbell doesn't come alone through the back door for his starting shift. Omar walks in behind him.

"Hey, Olivia. I'm just dropping him off, but he says you're too busy to go with us tonight and I wanted to twist your arm," Omar says, smiling broadly with his hands in praying pose in front of him.

"Umm," I say, vying for time because I have no damn idea what he's talking about and I don't want to call Campbell a liar. Clearly something is going on that he doesn't want me to be a part of. I'm smiling, but I hope Omar can't see how forced it is.

"Come on, Omar. She doesn't want to let you down," Campbell says, not looking at me, not giving me any hint at all as to what is going on.

"Yeah. Well, Campbell knows I have a special project and I need to work a lot lately, so," I say, with my face starting to burn, and less than a clear idea as to why I'm covering for my so very fake boyfriend.

"Tonight, though? You're here this morning, are you really

working tonight?" Omar asks, darting a speculative glance to his cousin.

"In the morning, yeah. I have to get up really early." I'm making excuses, biting my bottom lip, and not looking at him while I blush. I doubt he believes me, I don't believe me either.

"See? That's okay. We can still get you home in time for whatever you have to do so bad in the morning on a Sunday," Omar says, arms wide and smiling. "This is going to be great. You're going to love it. Plus, it will let Katie have her way."

Omar winks at me and turns to go, as if it's all settled.

"Ah," I squeak. I don't talk, just a high pitched croaking comes out of my mouth as my brain tries to make sense out of what just happened.

Omar waves and leaves out the back door, it swings shut and I'm left staring after him feeling decidedly hijacked.

"Campbell, what the hell did I just not at all agree to doing tonight?" I ask, boring a hole in the top of his head with my eyes while he stares at the just done tie on his apron.

"Olivia, I'm sorry about that," he says and heads to the walk in, leaving me still wondering with no answers.

I start my dough and the heat leaves my face, instead I can feel the pressure of angry, bitter tears threatening behind my eyes.

Yes, I was the one who said we should end this ridiculous attempt to get me to have a real life. And of course I'm thrilled it worked enough that I have people I talk to and eat lunch with at school every day, people I really do consider my friends, but this level of dismissal sucks.

The dough in front of me becomes a target, a perfect receptacle for my fists.

Pounding on the dough, again and again, mercilessly attacking it, I'm only stopped by Campbell's hands on mine.

"Stop," he says, his voice hushed, his eyes soft and inches from mine as he turns me toward him.

"Why?" I ask, at a loss for what all to say, there's too much roiling through my brain, and the only thing that comes out is a stupid half formed question, it makes me more mad and the tears flow freely, escaping past my lashes.

"You ruined the dough," he says, not taking his eyes from mine.

I look down at my hands, covered in globs of dough gone sticky and the misshapen mound of it on the table. His hands are on mine, getting gummed up too. Somehow, the mess of dough stops my burst of tears and I cough, finally able to speak.

"Oh. No, I mean why are you so angry with me? You won't even look at me." No matter that I can voice my frustration now, I still can't look at him. All the calm he normally brings is gone.

"Olivia, I'm not mad at you. You said you wanted distance from our little experiment. I was giving it to you," he says, his voice gruff.

He's right. I did say that. But this awkwardness, I never wanted that.

"Don't worry about me. We have to get this cleaned up and get to work," he says, leading me to the sink so we can wash our hands side by side.

A lot of flour later, I get the mess I made of the dough cleaned up. I can't make sense out of what's going on anymore, so I don't try. Campbell and I work through the morning routine to get ready for opening. As usual, but without any words to each other.

The unspoken words, my confusion at what I'm supposed to do about this problem I've caused by going along with this crazy scheme, wait in head. My hands don't shake by sheer force of will through my entire shift.

A half hour before we're supposed to get off of work, Campbell puts in an order for a bunch of pizzas. Obviously, whatever we're doing tonight doesn't include more of his aunt's incredible food.

"You ready?" he asks, standing by the back door with his many pies when I drop my apron into the laundry bin.

"Like this?" I ask, gesturing to my less than exciting plain white tee and jeans as I grab my jacket from the lockers.

"We're not going to the Space Needle," he says, trying to balance the boxes in his arms so he can open the door.

"I'll get it." The wind that comes in from the outside is bitterly cold. Whatever he thinks about my clothes, this is the wrong coat. But I shiver in silence as we go out to the parking lot.

His aunt's car is nowhere that I can see, and I'm wondering if we'll be walking to whatever destination he has in mind. But he leads me to a black classic car with flames painted on the hood and sets his pizzas on the roof while he fishes keys out of his pocket.

"This is the car you were looking at?" I ask, stepping back to take it all in. It's beautiful, and I don't know what I was expecting, but this isn't it.

"A 1960 Mercury Comet. I've always wanted a classic, and they aren't anything you can get on the island. If I drove more it wouldn't be practical at all, but this is a dream," he says, climbing in to lean across the mile of the front seat to unlock the passenger side.

Climbing into the cream interior, I realize the seats aren't leather like I thought, they're naugahide or something, worn soft with the years, but in great shape.

"How many miles does this thing have?" I ask when he starts the engine and it rumbles, smooth and throaty.

"It only has six thousand miles, which is amazing for its age.

I got it for two grand because the lady inherited it and didn't want a gas car that she thought didn't run. It just needed a new generator and voltage regulator."

He maneuvers us out of the parking lot, and I rub my hands together in front of the heater, that also works perfectly.

"This car is huge." The seat we're in is a long bench that's bigger than a twin bed, the back seat is the same. Parking this thing in the city would be a nightmare, good thing he walks a lot.

"Believe it or not, this is the super compact model," he says, and laughs.

"Now you're just messing with me."

"I swear, back in Luke's infancy, he was a small boy," he says, and pats the steering wheel.

"Luke?" I'm desperately trying not to laugh, but I'm smiling.

"Luke Spacecruiser." He nods, and I lose it, it's too much.

He smiles at me when he stops at a light.

"Check it out," he says, gesturing to the dash.

I look on the top of the massive dash and there's an antique license plate with the letters LUK on it.

"Luke." I'm laughing and shaking my head as he pulls into the parking lot of Seattle's Best Karaoke.

CHAPTER 22

"Okay, the food's here," Deacon says as we open the door to the room they've been given for the night.

"Thanks," Campbell says, putting the boxes onto the coffee table.

"He means you guys, but he's also dying of hunger because he's a big baby with a giant appetite," Katie says, waving me over to her on one of the couches.

"Olivia, I'm so excited for the next couple weeks. When are we going shopping?" she asks, jumping up to give me a hug.

"Next couple weeks?" I ask, smiling over her shoulder to say hi to the others on the couches.

"I haven't asked her yet," Campbell says right behind me.

He grabs my hips and squeezes between me and the coffee table to take a seat next to where Katie was, and my cheeks heat, knowing we're going to be in the same lap sitting position we were in last time. At least while everyone eats, and no one is standing up to sing.

Great. Because this isn't even more weird than it was last time or anything.

"Well, of course you're taking her; you don't have to ask. But I want to go shopping with her," Katie says, leaning over to grab a slice she hands to Campbell and one she hands to me.

Betty and Theresa are deep in a conversation about dresses as I take my seat on Campbell's lap, still not understanding what I so clearly should.

"Shopping for what?" I ask, trying again to have someone explain to me what is going on without coming right out and screaming at them that I have no idea what they're all talking about.

Katie laughs, until she stops and looks closer at me, her brows drawn down.

"You're serious?" she asks, and I roll my eyes.

"Damn, okay," she says, her eyes wide and brows way up now.

Maybe I put too much exasperation in my eye roll.

"Campbell, what the hell, dude?" Deacon asks, shaking his head.

"Olivia," Campbell says, putting one hand on mine. "Will you go with me to Katie and Deacon's eighteenth birthday party?" he asks.

"Wait, you guys are having a birthday party? Together?" I ask, both of them grinning like fools. "Am I invited?"

"Ridiculous question, of course you are. Pay attention to the man, he asked you a question," Deacon says, gesturing to Campbell who is wearing an amused smile.

"Oh, right. Of course, I'll go with you," I say to general cheers.

"Why is this such a big deal?" I ask Campbell, leaning into him so I can ask quietly.

"It's a black tie affair," Campbell says, with a small shake of his head.

"My darling, Campbell, this is so much better than that,"

Katie says, reaching into her bag and pulling out two aqua glass bottles with corks in the top and handing them to us.

"This is a very Bond moment, and you're going to be thanking us," Deacon says, and winks.

"Definitely," Katie says, raising a brow and grinning in a decidedly devilish way.

Campbell pops the cork on his bottle and pulls out a rolled up scroll with gold and black lettering, I follow his lead and read my own.

It's a very regal looking announcement for the eighteenth birthdays of Deacon King Jefferson and Katherine Holiday Baxter-Jefferson on board the Tech-Giant, a private yacht docked in the sound.

"This is kind of incredible," I say, thinking out loud.

"Not as impressive as it looks; my Pop did work for the guy who owns the boat, Deacon's dad is taking care of the food, and our entire family is crafting their way into oblivion making the decorations. We can make random crap look fancy as hell," Katie says, and we all laugh at how not black tie her statement is.

"I think I'm going to enjoy watching you try to be formal for a whole night," I say.

"Oh, she can turn it on when she wants, but this won't be stuffy. Just damn good looking fun," Deacon says.

"Which is why you need to go shopping with me," Katie says, bouncing in her seat and pulling on the leg of my jeans.

"Okay, okay. We'll go shopping," I say, and open my eyes wide to Campbell, trying to ask him what he's thinking in all of this insanity.

"Don't look to me for help. I can't save you from her, and she told me I have to get a suit," Campbell says with a smile.

The look on Katie's face as she smiles at me and Campbell

makes me suspect there's more than just shopping on her mind for me for this party.

"You're both going to love it," she says.

CHAPTER 23

"This is going to be great. I know we'll find the perfect outfit for you here," Katie says, opening the door to a boutique the following Saturday.

All the girls invited to the party have been looking at pictures of dresses online all week while I've been looking up different ways to prepare clams and calamari for my pizza topping.

I love dresses, and dressing up, but this feels like such a big distraction for me right now. Like what I should be focusing on is at home in the kitchen in the shape of a pizza not a shop in an a-line.

The boutique has rough wood floors, mirrored tables, and walls in a black brocade wall paper with massive white trim everywhere. It's intimidating in its chicness.

"I think I'm looking for something simple," I say, immediately overwhelmed by the sheer number of options. Maybe I should have done a little online searching too.

"No. We're going to find you something that's going to kill Campbell. That boy's got it so bad already; wait till I'm done.

He'll never be the same," she says, pulling me further into the store by the hand.

"You make this sound like an epic quest, you're Don Quixote, and my love life is your city of gold." My voice gets quieter as I say more to myself than to her, "I think you might be tilting at windmills."

"I know that's a literary reference, but I'm going into engineering." She combs through the racks and looks me up and down, calculating.

"Why can't you like literature and engineering?" I ask, touching a soft, gauzy fabric of a skirt.

"Oh, people can, just not me. Unless it's high fantasy or sci-fi, ooh, what about this one?" she asks, pulling a red dress down and holding it up to me.

"Red? I don't know." People who are guaranteed to blush, like me, probably should stay away from reds.

"It would look great on you. But we'll grab a bunch more; what size are you?" she asks, and grabs so many options from the racks around us, I get dizzy after I tell her my size.

"You know what we should do?" she asks, once she shoves me in a dressing room to start the parade of trying on she insists I share with her.

"Get you into some of these?" I ask, shimmying into a deep green, body skimming one.

"I have mine, but you need shoes." Her voice trails off and I imagine her wandering away to find me some. How she thinks we can choose shoes without knowing the dress, I have no idea.

The curtain is yanked back before I can make grab for it, and for a second, I can't breathe. Until I remember I already have the dress on, and it's only Katie.

"Oh, no. That dress is fine, but we can do better. And here, try these on with whatever you put on next. They're divine," she says, handing me a box.

"How did you know my shoe size?" I ask the already closed curtain as I look at the box.

"Just a good guess." Her voice floats to me through the dressing room, but I'm barely aware because the shoes she hands me are the most stunning pair I've ever seen.

I put them on the floor and discard half the dresses in the room with me, knowing I have to wear these shoes and none of them go with them at all.

But the red one she picked when we first walked into the store would, and against my better judgement, I take it off the hanger.

It skims the floor, which I don't care for because it covers up the shoes, but the tiny polk-a-dots in the tulle of the skirt are nice, even if I'm not sure about the spaghetti strap top.

The curtain of the dressing room makes a swish sound when I push it back and step out into the waiting area where Katie sits, looking at her phone.

"Wow." Her phone is forgotten in her hand as I make my way to the three-way mirror.

She's right, this looks great on me. I feel like a different person, someone more carefree, the lightness of the skirt makes me feel like I'm floating.

"Campbell is going to fall over," she says, standing over my shoulder looking at the mirrors with me.

Heat floods my chest and my face, that she's being so nice, and I haven't told her the truth about Campbell and me.

"Oh, no. Not red. It looks incredible, but your blush is so cute and now you look splotchy," she says, grabbing me so I only get a glimpse of what she's talking about, and shoving me toward the dressing room.

"I tried to warn you," I say, through the closed curtain as I try on a silver dress that at least the shoes show with.

Trying to get out to the mirrors with this one is almost

impossible and Katie's laughing and shooing me away before I get there.

"That's a no on the pencil skirts," I say, hopping out of the dress again.

In front of me there are only a few left and only one that wouldn't cover up the shoes, so I go with that one next. The shoes are something I want to show off.

Opening up the curtain this time makes Katie drop her phone, like her hands forgot how to work. She leaves it behind in her seat, coming to stand over my shoulder again as I stare at the girl in the mirrors. I know she's me, but the normally nondescript aspects of my face are suddenly pretty. My hair looks rich, my eyes warm. My skin, even the blush creeping up my neck looks like I'm glowing.

The shoes, bright red, open toed heels that tie around my ankles in oversized bows make my legs look dainty by comparison. The dress is white on the top, in a satin that shines, with thick straps and a sweetheart neckline. The skirt is white satin with a black tulle overlay that bells out and makes my waist look tiny.

"You're a dream," Katie says, a wistful smile on her face.

And it's true, I am. A dream for the wrong guy.

CHAPTER 24

The night of the party I have to get off of work early, and so does Campbell. He smiles at me all night, touching my hand whenever I start to get nervous. I know he's trying to calm me, but it does the opposite tonight.

I don't know what we're doing anymore. This whole thing seemed like a good idea at the time and now it feels like a lie. Part of me is afraid that my friends have gone to so much trouble to help Campbell and I work, when for it to work we need to not end up together, that they might not forgive me.

One of Junior's friends comes in twenty minutes before we're supposed to get off of work to help with washing the dishes, and Dad hasn't come downstairs yet. His friend has hair longer than mine tied up in a knot on his head and a thick beard.

I hate beards, I've seen too many men spill crumbs into them and not know they're sporting bits of pizza as decoration when they walk out the door for me to like them. Maybe if more guys wiped their beards when they were done eating, they wouldn't bug me. But Junior's friend immediately makes me want to look away.

My apron string is caught and doesn't want to untie but behind me I hear Campbell giving instructions to the temporary dishwasher. It's odd because everyone else here will be able to point Junior's friend in the right direction if he gets into the weeds in the kitchen; it's not like he's cooking.

"No, I'm serious. I don't care what Junior has told you; this is important," Campbell's voice says from behind me.

I yank on my apron and spin to face him.

He's turning away from my brother's friend and heading toward me without looking up so he almost walks right into me, I don't move.

"Oh, sorry Olivia," he says, grabbing the tails of my apron out of my hands and deftly untying it with his long fingers. "As soon as I get ready, I'll be back here to pick you up."

"It won't take long, an hour, okay?" I say, breathless now that my face is starting to heat and I'm having trouble reminding myself that this is the same group of people we've hung out with before. They already like me, I shouldn't be worried.

Campbell drops the ends of my apron and looks me in the eyes, his face softens, and he put a hand on my shoulder.

"This is going to be fun. I promise. Just think of it as another night at Seattle's Best." He smiles and walks out the door.

Just another karaoke night. No big deal.

I keep my reminders on repeat as I head up to our apartment.

Nothing to worry about.

The door to our apartment opens on a surrealist painting. Mom is swaying in her seat in the living room to one of the awful boy band songs of her childhood.

"What are you doing?" I ask, barely audible over the din.

"Olivia, hurry, go get in the shower," she says, not answering any of the million questions running through my head.

I do need to take a shower and get ready, but if the cancer has spread to her brain and this is a symptom, I probably should cancel. Instead of listening to her command, I join her on the couch, and she takes my hand, swinging it wildly in time to the music.

"Angela, please," Dad says, turning the music down. "Oh, Livvy, glad you're here, you can talk some sense into her. She wants to help you get ready, but she needs to take it easy."

Mom freezes and drops my hand, she stands up, none of her usual unsteadiness showing, and stares at him, her head tilted back, nose in the air, and a thousand ovens worth of heat pouring out of her eyes.

"You telling me what to do again, Joe?" she asks.

He freezes, his hand outstretched, and shakes his head, slowly, side to side.

"Good. You have work," Mom says.

Oof, Dad. Go, seriously, I try to say with my eyes. A dismissal in Mom speak isn't a choose your own adventure, it's a damn order to get out of her face.

He glances at me and seems to understand, because he sighs and leaves.

Mom sits back onto the sofa and smiles at me like nothing at all just went on between her and Dad.

"Hurry, Livvy, you don't have a lot of time and I want to do your hair and makeup for you," she says, patting my hand in a gentle shove toward my room.

I do as I'm told, the strangeness of whatever has possessed my mother chasing me to finish up and get back to her in record time without any nerves slowing me down.

Wearing panties and a bra under a towel wrapped around my body and another wrapped around my hair, I peek out the door of my room to find Mom still waiting for me on the couch. And she's still dancing.

"Okay, Livvy, since we don't have a lot of time, I'm going to brush out your hair and set in these curlers," Mom says, pulling my hand to sit me on the ottoman in front of her seat on the couch, "then we'll do your makeup and finish your hair last." She pulls my towel from my head and dragging the brush through my hair.

It's been years since my Mom has brushed my hair, and her ability to do it efficiently while not pulling at the tangles is a miracle of home that catches in my throat. She hums while she does it and I reach a hand back to touch her knee.

"This party is like a prom, isn't it?" she asks, her voice full of joy.

"Yeah, and," I say, stopping when I realize I was about to blurt out much more to her than I think she should have to deal with right now.

"And, what, Livvy?"

"Prom isn't," I pause to take a breath and then finish, "really something I know how to do," I say, while she rolls my hair around warm curlers and pins them in place on my head.

"Baby, there isn't anything to know. Dances are just another way to hang out with your friends, formal dances are just that with better outfits. Formal anything is really just an excuse to wear fancy clothes and use your good manners until no one can hear you but the people that won't mind if you still swear or tell a dirty joke."

"Mom."

She laughs and it makes me laugh too, chasing away the heaviness of her doing my hair. She finishes the rollers and turns me around on the ottoman to do my makeup.

"Just don't make me look like a different person," I say, shutting my eyes.

"How would I do that?"

"There are some crazy things people can do with makeup according to youtube. There's this guy who makes himself into all kinds of famous people, from Martha Stewart to Audrey Hepburn. It's amazing."

"Well, he's not here, and while I know what I'm doing, I don't have the slightest idea how to do that and wouldn't want to. You're beautiful as is."

"Mom."

She laughs again and I smile. We've missed so much of this, the kind of time and space to be with each other and do normal things together. Even if this isn't totally normal, it's nice.

"Joe tells me Campbell is nice and has really been working hard; he wants to teach him how to throw soon."

My eyes pop open and she's grinning at me.

"Dear god, no. Please, Mom," I say, and she points to my eyes.

I take a deep breath and shut my eyes again.

"Why don't you want him to learn to throw?" she asks.

"It isn't that, and you know it. I just don't want Dad interrogating him. Why don't we train him to be a server first?" I'm trying to think fast and come up with some plausible way out for Campbell and me.

"Okay, but I think you should do something to help him out if you're going to throw him to the wolves of the customers," she says.

"What do you mean, help him out?"

"Campbell deserves to be respected and not to have anyone misgender him, don't you think?" she asks, it sends my mind spinning.

She's right. He shouldn't have to introduce himself as he/him to everyone and have it be a way to be immediately outed.

"He didn't have to tell me he's trans, he introduced himself with his pronouns and I knew. So," I say, thinking harder about a way for it to be normalized for all of us, even cis me.

"What if I made up new nametags for everyone with our pronouns on them?" I ask, and can't help smiling because I think it will work.

"That's a lovely idea."

CHAPTER 25

*W*hen Mom is finished and I've put on my killer shoes and great dress, I feel like a different person, even if I just look like a much prettier version of myself.

"You have to come out here and show me before he gets here. I need to double check," Mom calls from the living room, her voice filtered through my door and the music off, replaced with the low tones of some show on the TV.

My hair is pinned back from my face in the front, creating a half updo with the rest falling in loose curls down my back and a few framing my face. With my outfit, I look like the kind of girl who would never have so many scars on her hands and arms from pizza ovens.

The look on Mom's face as I walk into the living room makes my heart beat faster. Her hand is on her heart, her head tilted, her eyes soft and watering and her smile adoring.

"Livvy, you're stunning," she says, her voice quiet, and she dabs at the corner of one eye.

"Mom," I say, my face heating.

At least I don't have to stand around and grow ever more

embarrassed by her attention, because the outside doorbell rings.

"He's here," I say, and I can't move. I have to go to the door and let him in, but I can't, my legs are raw dough, unable to hold their shape.

"Mom," I say, and she levers herself to her feet, shuffling past me to the door.

"Hello, Campbell, it's so nice to meet you. I'm Angela, she/her," Mom says, her voice not betraying any concern about the scarf covering her bald head, or the sweatpants and sweatshirt she's wearing covered in her thick sweater-coat, and not even her leopard print fuzzy slippers. She may as well be a grand lady answering the door, instead of my sick mother in her uniform of comfort.

"Hello, Angela, it's nice to meet you too. Is Olivia ready?" he asks.

She steps to the side and gestures him in the door.

Campbell is in a suit that looks like it was made specifically for him in a dark grey with deep green shirt, tie, and pocket square. In his hand he has a red rose.

When he spots me, his mouth drops open and his eyes widen, his hand with the rose falls limp to his side the rose itself pointing at the floor.

"I like your suit, the green is a good color on you," I say, trying to find anything to say that won't make me feel like the biggest dating noob on the planet.

"He-" he starts, coughs and raises the rose, holding it out toward me, "here, this is for you."

"Thank you," I say, taking it from him while I bury the thought he thinks I look like crap because he didn't say anything.

"Livvy, I'll get that into some water so you two can head out. I thought you could wear this," Mom says, taking the rose from me and replacing it with a black cashmere wrap.

"I love this, Mom. Thank you," I say, kissing her on the cheek. It isn't a lie; her cashmere wrap is one of the clothing items I used to steal to play dress up with from her closet when I was little.

Campbell rushes to my side and takes the wrap from me to place it around my shoulders.

"Don't worry about a curfew for tonight. Dad has tomorrow morning covered. I've given you both the day off with pay," Mom says.

"Mom, what?"

She grabs my hand and kisses me on the cheek.

"Let me spoil you this one time, okay?"

"Thank you, Angela," Campbell says.

Tears are building at the back of my eyes so I have to take a deep breath and focus on the smile I'm giving my mom as he puts his hand on the small of my back and leads me out the door and to his waiting car.

He opens the door for me and closes it behind me once I'm inside.

We don't say a word to each other while he navigates through the city, bringing us to where the boat is docked. Every second feels like the static electricity of the wait for him to speak gets stronger until I wonder if my hair is starting to stand on end.

"Before," he starts, but coughs and clears his throat and starts again. "Um, before we get there, I wanted to say that your mom seems really nice, and you," he turns and looks at me and looks back at the road in front of us, "you look incredible."

A breath I was only partially aware I was holding pours out of my mouth in a rush.

"I…" I realize too late that I shouldn't say anything, and just leave my started comment hanging instead of being smart and covering for myself while my face catches fire in a blush.

"You, what?" he asks, gently.

Too late now, I need to answer him and let him know I am profoundly stupid for saying anything at all.

"I thought you didn't like my dress," I say.

"Why the hell would you think that?" he asks, as he pulls the car into a parking spot at the marina.

"You didn't say anything when you saw me is all, but thank you for the compliment," I say, looking at my hands, curled into each other on my lap.

"The thing is, I couldn't speak," he says, and I look up at him smiling at me. "No one has ever made me forget my own name before, but you did."

My blush is creeping up to my eyebrows now, but I don't care for a minute.

He clears his throat and turns off the car.

"Let's go; Omar is going to fall overboard when he sees you," he says and climbs out.

Omar. I almost forgot.

Campbell opens the door for me and the wintery air off the water smells of salt and seagrass as he leads me down to the ship for the party. It's already started, the noise of music and people laughing floats to us on the dock.

We walk up a ramp into the boat and into a throng of people I don't know, the faces of our friends not immediately in sight starts my hands to shaking.

He takes one of my hands. His are warm and solid, his calm spreading over me as we make our way through the crowd looking for someone familiar.

A squeal rings through the air behind us and we turn to find Katie darting around people in her gown, coming straight at us.

"I'm so glad you're here," she says, taking my other hand and squeezing it.

"Here, let me get someone to put that at our table," she goes on, grabbing the wrap from my shoulders, handing it to someone, and barking orders at them while I reach for it with the hand still trapped by Campbell's.

"Come on, I want you to meet everyone," Katie says, dragging me, and Campbell by default, along behind her toward some unknown destination in the crowd.

Theresa and Rebecca are the first people I see through the crowd. Theresa looks soft and warm in a velvet burgundy dress with an exposed back that Rebecca is trailing her hand along. It sends goosebumps up my own as I watch her hand caress my ex-girlfriend's skin.

Rebecca is like some sort of television assassin in a corseted little black dress with thigh high boots.

If they're not careful the crowd of football players around them are going to start drooling.

Deacon is among the crowd but he's laughing at something they said, looking totally unaware of the effect they're having on the guys around him.

"He really is pure," I say, Katie pulling on my hand snorts a laugh.

"My cousin is the best of us," Katie says, stopping to twirl on me with a finger raised. "Never tell him I said so."

"Your secret is safe," Campbell says behind me while I laugh.

Katie lets go of my hand to pounce on Deacon, clinging to

his neck while she hangs on his back like he's a pony ride at the supermarket and she's five.

"Ah, okay. I'll get you a drink, you loon. Get off me," Deacon says, laughing as she dismounts.

"Happy birthday to us," she yells after him as he walks away shaking his head.

"We missed something," Campbell says.

"She's been haranguing him to get her a drink for half an hour. Hi, guys. I like the look, Olivia," Omar says, and I realize I missed him standing there.

"Oh, thank you. I didn't think the apron would work for the occasion," I say, and earn a few chuckles from the people around me.

"The best table is right over there," Katie says, pointing past the group toward the front table to the right of the stage.

"Is there going to be a band?" I ask, looking at the stage with some equipment on it.

"Yes, and later we have a surprise. The band will start in a few minutes, until then we just have a few songs. When the band starts, though, I want to see my babies take to the dance floor," Katie says, her eyebrows wiggling up and down.

"Babies?" Campbell asks, a huge smile on his face and one eyebrow raised.

"Campbell, you and Olivia are my babies now, don't fight it." Katie reaches up to pat him on the head, but he ducks out from under her hand, his arm raising to protect his hair and I crack up laughing.

"The hair, Katie. Don't mess with the hair," he says, making everyone laugh.

We make our way over to the table and I take a seat at the chair that has my wrap draped across the back, leaving the others behind.

"Not so bad, although if Katie makes a move for my hair again, she's going overboard," he says.

"I don't know how I got here, but I kind of like being Katie's baby," I say, thinking that I could have a much worse mother for my entrance to the world of being social. My hands aren't shaking anymore, and the whole evening feels like a much better idea than it did twenty minutes ago.

"Don't let her hear you say that," Deacon says as he takes a seat across from me with a heaping plate in front of him.

"Why not?" I ask, and Campbell squeezes my hand with a smile.

"She'll start in with the grand plans of how to improve your life. Trust me, no good can come from that. She means well, but she gets a little…" Deacon trails off and pops a shrimp into his mouth, ending whatever he was going to say.

Before I can ask for him to continue, the band starts up and the boat begins to pull away from the dock.

"Come on," Campbell says, pulling me to my feet and over to the railing to watch the city lights fade into a string of romantic fairy lights as we move out into the water.

"It's beautiful. Sometimes I forget, living in the middle of it," I say, and shiver as the cold comes off the water, touching me now that we're not in the crush of so many people.

"Are you cold?" he asks, putting an arm around me and sharing his body heat with me.

"Not now, thank you," I say, looking up at him, the light from the party behind us highlighting the soft contours of his cheekbones and jawline. But, his jawline looks different than when I picture him in my head.

I reach out a hand and trail a finger along his jaw, he closes his eyes at my touch.

"You look different," I say, my voice quiet, the sound of the band pounding behind us.

"Testosterone, it's starting to change things. It's taken a year," he says, and sighs.

"Are you happy with the changes?" I ask, I don't want to tell him that no matter what he looks like, I think he's beautiful. Not if he doesn't think so.

"Yes, I've waited my whole life," he says.

"I'm happy for you. I like your face both ways," I say, trying to explain to him what I mean, hoping he understands that I'm not trying to be insensitive to his feelings.

He smiles and hugs me, enveloping me completely in his warmth, and I know he does understand my support of him.

"Okay, babies, this next song is for you, get out here," Katie calls over all the music.

Campbell pulls back from me, smiling, and rolls his eyes.

"We better get out there and dance or I don't think she'll stop," he says.

The dance floor is pulsating with the movements of the guests, some great dancers like Katie, some trying not to embarrass themselves like me, and some who desperately need help like Omar.

"What is your cousin doing?" I ask, leaning into Campbell's ear, as Omar tries and fails to find the beat.

"He's committing a crime," Campbell says, shaking his head.

I'm laughing so hard I have to lean on Campbell, but Katie is making her way over to Omar.

She joins him in the dance, planting his hands on her hips and she forces his body to move in rhythm to the music. It doesn't take long for them to turn into the sexiest moving couple on the dance floor.

"Damn she's good," Campbell says, and I swallow around a suddenly dry throat.

There's no way he can be that bad and do those moves minutes later, unless he was faking it to get her attention. She can't stop herself from trying to help someone making a fool of themselves. Maybe she's just being the social Mom and he really is that fast a learner, maybe –

Nope. They're kissing.

I freeze and around me people start cheering them on. The music changes to a slow song, they stop kissing but now they're staring into each other's eyes, swaying in a world of their own.

Campbell pulls me to his chest, forcing me out of my shock to sway with me to the song.

"Olivia," he says and stops.

Just my name, nothing more. What is there to say, really? Whatever game we've been playing, I just lost.

"Guys," Katie calls, her and Omar have made their way to us, his arm around her and they take up position, dancing next to us. "Now we can go on a double date."

Omar is staring at her like she is all the stars in the sky, and I don't know what do, let alone what to say.

"That would be great," Campbell says, saving me from this moment.

"Now go away, please," I say, not meaning to open my mouth and so shocked when I do my whole body stops, I even forget to breathe for a second.

"What?" Katie says, laughing the kind of trying really hard to not take that personal laugh I am intimately familiar with because it's usually coming out of me.

"I feel inspired and want to do something about it," Campbell says, covering for me again, although I don't catch on to what he means.

Not until he takes a hand off my hip to touch a finger to my chin. He turns my face to his and smiles his half smile at me, closes his eyes and touches his lips to mine.

I stare at his closed lids for a beat, unable to believe this is really happening, then I remember I'm supposed to close my eyes too.

With my eyes closed I feel the kiss, the light pressure of his sweet kiss, his saving of me. His lips are soft and my heart stutters, my stomach fluttering, and I sink into him. I open my lips and invite him to deepen the kiss with my tongue on his lips. He does, his kisses turn greedy and his hand on the small of my back presses me against him harder while his other hand cups the side of my neck, his thumb running along my jaw, his fingers buried in the hair at the nape of my neck.

He pulls away from me and I'm drunk, not fully aware of the music or the people around us whooping and cheering us on. The only thing I'm completely aware of is the warmth of his brown eyes, the beauty of the flecks of green in them, and how badly I want to kiss him again.

I pull his face back to mine and get what I want.

CHAPTER 27

The night feels charged with my own physical need. Campbell doesn't go more than twenty minutes without my mouth on his, the urge strikes me at the oddest moments. When he takes a drink and his lips perfectly touch the glass, when someone makes a joke and he throws his head back and laughs, when he smiles with half his mouth, every time he smiles with half his mouth, I want to drown in him. Any anxiety I had is buried in his eyes and his lips, the touch of his hand, and how much I wish we were alone.

As we head into the harbor the entire party crowds the railings to watch the light change as we enter the circle of city ambiance again.

I'm standing in front of Campbell, my wrap around me, protecting me from the cold, and his arms holing it in place, his head resting on my shoulder. I turn my head and kiss him again, holding his arms against me.

"Damn, I'm surprised Olivia is so..." Rebecca says, louder than I think she intends as her voice trails into hushed murmurs.

Campbell stops kissing me, putting his forehead to mine.

"I'm not," Theresa says, she's the only one here who would know.

And just like that, I figure it out. This isn't fake, not anymore, not for me.

Katie and Omar are good together. I'm happy for them, but I'm happier for me. Campbell is so much better than what I thought I wanted, he's more than a rebound. He could be very real.

We say our goodbyes, hugging our friends, saying another happy birthday to Deacon and Katie, and make our way to Campbell's car, his hand in mine.

He opens the car door for me, and we get in. Pulling out of the lot, he says, "I'm sorry. I thought tonight would end differently."

The rocking motion of the boat that's still in my abdomen turns into a tidal wave.

"You're sorry?" I ask, hoping he will say something else, clarify his words so the boat of my heart isn't capsized.

"Omar should have ended up with you tonight. I had this plan in my head of a way to make it work for you to get what you wanted. I'm sorry you didn't." His hands are both on his giant steering wheel, wringing it out like a wet rag.

"I…" I start, there are no words to say to him. There's no way to admit how happy I am that I didn't get what I thought I wanted, not now. We have to still work together. We have to see each other all the time, even if I avoid hanging out with the group after school. All my half formed ideas of being with him start shriveling up like toppings left out overnight.

Anger at myself for being so stupid as to think he would really be interested in me beyond friendship builds, my hands start shaking and tears drip down my face.

Not now. Not now, damn it. Stupid, useless, tears, I'll look like a fool.

"Olivia, please don't cry," he says, "not over my stupid cousin. I'm sorry this didn't work. I really thought it would." He reaches across the mile of seat between us to touch my hand and that does it.

"I'm not crying over him, you idiot," I say, swiping at my tears, trying in vain to will them away.

"Are those angry tears?" he asks, stopping at a light and handing me his pocket square.

I swipe it out of his hand and blot my cheeks, trying not to ruin the fantastic makeup my mother did for me.

"Of course, they're angry tears. I'm angry at myself." I start mumbling to myself, trying to talk my way to stopping the tears. "I'm so stupid. Why would he want to be with me? He was just trying to be nice to me."

"Lots of people want to be with you. You don't see the way people look at you. You're amazing," he says, pulling into the back lot of the restaurant.

"You don't want to be with me," I say, blurting out what I'm thinking and slamming my hands over my mouth so nothing else leaks out.

"Uh... I... What?" he stammers.

The door flies open once my scrambling fingers get a hold on the handle and I fling myself from the car, darting through the empty lot to the stairs and running up them to my house.

My tears blind me as I try to be as silent as possible making my way to my room. By some miracle my house is already asleep or still in the restaurant.

In my room, behind the protection of my door, I fling myself on my bed. Tears pour from my eyes to dampen one of my superfluous pillows. The pillow is the green one, the exact shade of the flecks in Campbell's eyes. My hand snaps out, flinging it. It thumps against the wall and lands on my desk. Sitting up, I realize the whole new color scheme of my décor is like Campbell's eyes. Warm copper and brown, cream and touches of green.

Ugly, outdated lilac looks so much better right now than this torture chamber of beautiful perfection.

My phone, ignored as usual, chimes from its place on my desk.

Whoever wants to me to come in tomorrow for them can shut the hell up. My plans are to cry until I forget that the bedding I'm hiding in looks like Campbell's eyes.

The chime comes again, and I turn off my light.

I don't bother to take off my shoes, or climb out of my dress. They'll be ruined by the morning, but right now I don't care. The wrap becomes a blanket as I don't have the will to climb into the covers.

The chime sounds again.

Even now, when I should be given a pass, the restaurant won't leave me alone.

And again. The sound becomes a haunting thing, ominous and loaded, devoid of all the false cheer the high pitched ding ding usually holds.

It won't stop. By the tenth damn time I fling the wrap off of me and go to retrieve my phone in the dark, prepared to call the person back and scream.

But my screen shows one text from Katie and more than a dozen from Campbell.

Katie's text is just a check in and hope that I had fun, with a lip emoji.

Campbell's texts are a bomb waiting for me to cut the wrong wire. Staring at the image on my screen I know that if I open them and see something worse than what's already happened,

I'm going to have a hard time working with him. But if I don't check, I doubt I'll be able to sleep.

My hands shake, the screen blurring in front of me and I chuck the phone onto my bed.

I take the time to undress and throw on an over-sized tee-shirt, since I'm already up, before I climb into my covers and grab my phone again, to turn the damn thing off.

The chime sounds while it's in my hand, the accursed thing somehow knowing I was going to silence it and wanting to torture me one last time.

Fine.

My shaking fingers tap the screen before I can think through what I'm doing. His texts come to life.

Olivia, what did you mean in the car?

It would be a lot easier if you would talk to me, I don't know what's going on.

What you said… I'm confused.

You're mad at yourself? Why? Katie and Omar are your friends. Really. I know they are. They didn't know you wanted Omar because of my stupid plan.

Are you mad at me because it backfired? I understand if you are, but please don't hate me. I really thought it would work.

Is it the kissing? Are you upset because I kissed you? I really wasn't trying to take advantage of the situation, I thought it would make Omar jealous. Maybe. I don't know.

Please text me back. I don't want to call and wake up your mom.

Olivia, I'm still in my car in the parking lot. I don't know if I can sleep without hearing that you're okay.

You are okay, right? I know you're not really okay, but you know what I mean.

Tonight was supposed to be fun, it was supposed to be the

big night for you and Omar to get together. I'm sorry I screwed it up.

I put the phone down on my bed, and stare toward my window facing the back lot, wondering if Campbell is still out there.

Getting out of bed in the dark, I go to the window on the back curve of the turret, the only one I can maybe see his car from.

He's there. His impossible to miss car is in the pool of light from the street light at the edge of the lot.

On bare feet I leave my room, a ghost floating through my house in the night, and walk through the silence to the front door. The chill of the air outside stings on my cheeks where I realize tracks of tears have left them damp. The grooves in the wood of the steps become directional in my mind, guiding me to keep going on this foolish errand that can only end badly for my heart, but I can't keep reading texts, crying, and doing nothing to change this. At least I can send Campbell home, he might flee from my advances instead of leaving in peace, but I can't sleep knowing he's down here.

My phone chimes in my hand as I walk across the gritty blacktop, he probably hasn't seen me in the dark.

Inside the car he sits with his head down, the faint light from the screen of his phone shining up onto his face. A lock of his hair is hanging in front of him and I want to push it back so he can see clearly.

Walking into the light from the street lamp feels like my steps themselves are illuminated, gilded. The last steps of my path to heartache is paved in silver.

Feet from his car he looks up and his mouth drops open. He scrambles from the car, pulling off his jacket and runs to me to toss it around my shoulders.

"What are you doing? You'll freeze," he says, his hands

through his jacket the only warmth I feel where they rest on my upper arms.

"You need to know," I say, my voice stronger than it seems like it should sound right now.

"Need to know? Olivia," he says, his mouth opening and closing one whatever he wants to say.

"I don't want Omar, I wasn't mad that he and Katie are together now. I was mad at myself for not realizing that I am crazy about you," I say, my voice picking up speed as I say the words, like they're trying to outrun the consequences of putting them out into the world.

"But… you…" he says, his hands falling from my arms to his sides as he stares at me.

I nod, because that's what I thought, and take his coat off, placing it in his hand. Turning around, the surface of the lot scrapes against my bare feet like sand paper and I know I'll feel it tomorrow.

His jacket is draped around my shoulders again and he moves to stand in front of me again.

"Really?" he asks, half his mouth in the smile I adore.

"Yes."

Campbell pulls me into his arms, his body against mine like comfort food to my heart. Then his lips are on mine and my mouth is greedy, needing more and more.

CHAPTER 28

"Olivia, it's too cold. You have to go inside, and you're not wearing anything," he says, after he pulls his mouth away from mine and touches my forehead with his.

"I don't want to," I say and hold him closer.

"You're going to kill me," he says, grinning and kissing my neck.

A sound escapes me, some mixture of a moan and a sigh. He should never stop kissing my neck, but he does with a growl low in his throat.

"Come on," he says, tucking me under his arm as he walks me to my door. "The last thing I want is for your dad or Junior to come out here and see us. And I'm losing my ability to say no to you, so you need to go inside."

"Do you want to come in?" I ask, and swallow hard after I realize what my question suggests. But he laughs and kisses my cheek.

"More than you can imagine, but I think we should call it a night. Neither of us wants to face the assumptions in the morning," he says.

"I meant to sleep," I say. "Well, and kiss."

He stops on the step before the landing to my front door and kisses me again, proving that my plan of kissing and sleeping is a good one.

"You go on in. If I come in there, I'll forget how to be a gentleman and I don't want to screw this up," he says, cupping my cheek with his free hand and kissing me again.

"Good night, Campbell," I say and go inside my house, watching out the sidelight of the front door until he's back in his car and driving out the lot.

His jacket is still on my shoulders. It smells of winter chill and peaches and it comes with me back to bed.

Mom wakes me up in the morning, sitting on the end of my bed.

"Well?" she asks, eyeing the jacket draped across my chest and smiling.

"It was," I start and then pause, because I have no idea how to describe it all, how to explain that even the parts that hurt seem like a good thing after the gift of Campbell and I in the parking lot. "Perfect."

"Livvy, I'm so happy. This is exactly what I wanted when I said you needed to get out and do more. And look, you found Campbell." She pats my leg through the covers and is still grinning as she carefully pushes herself to standing and shuffles her way to my door.

I jump from the bed and go after her, standing close enough to catch her if she stumbles, and far enough I won't get in her way if she wants to go to the couch on her own.

Once she's comfortably situated on the couch with a movie on and her tea at her side, I head back to my room to get ready for the day. I don't have a plan for it, but I know it will include Campbell, and his lips.

After I'm showered, dressed, and in my room with the phone ringing Campbell, I'm also starving and I have a great idea.

"Good morning," he says, his voice thick and I imagine him still in bed. Sometimes the imagination is a beautiful thing.

"Good morning, sleepy head. I was hoping to go to breakfast. Do you know anyone who would, I don't know, maybe want to go with me?"

"I'll be there in fifteen minutes."

He hangs up the phone as I giggle. That's a quick turn around from sleeping to at my door, but I look at the time on the phone to see if he makes it.

Flopping back onto my bed with my phone I make another call. When I hang up, I realize what the date is, I have eight days left until the contest. My plan for today has to work. If it doesn't, I'll just pull an all nighter in the restaurant since it will be closed at eight tonight because it's Sunday.

A few minutes later I remember I need the saffron from the pantry in the restaurant and dart toward the stairs. My mother waves at me as I smile in passing. When I reach the bottom, I stop and peak out of the stairwell, not wanting to get caught by anyone, especially not Junior or Dad who will try and put me to work. It will look bad for my case to run the restaurant if they think I don't actually need this day off.

Nelson won't rat me out and I see him making dough; I can't see where Junior and Dad are, so they must be done with the chop. The restaurant isn't open yet, so they can't be with customers. They're probably slacking or cleaning up something they should have done last night.

Creeping out of the stairwell and heading to the pantry I give the shhh finger in front my mouth motion to Nelson who smiles and shakes his head at me.

Inside the pantry, I pull down my box of saffron and hear Junior's voice come from the kitchen just outside the door.

There is no good place to hide in here, but I squeeze against the shelves and slowly move toward the open door to the kitchen.

"No, Dad. I think this is a good idea. If I win this competition than Mom will stop fighting giving me the restaurant," Junior says.

Competition? Junior's words freeze me in tracks and all the blood drains from my body. I feel light headed. He can't mean the competition I'm working on.

"Well, I'm not saying it's a bad idea, I just don't know how you're going to come up with a new pizza in a week," Dad says.

Stepping out of the pantry, I'm in the cold place again. My anger isn't causing tears today, just icy indifference tinged with disgust. My dad is helping my brother try to rob me again.

"There's no way you're going to be able to come up with an original idea that quickly, even with Dad's help," I say, to their shocked faces. "Besides, it would be a win only for you, because I already entered the competition under the restaurant's name months ago. Nice try, though. I'm sure Mom will love hearing about your scheming."

Dad is spluttering behind me and Junior is calling my name, but I don't stop, turn, or acknowledge them in any way. I head back upstairs to my mother to embrace the little sister tattle-tale role. They can both get burnt.

In our family room, my mom is on the couch with a book and the television on.

"Mom, I entered a best pizza competition under the restaurant's name," I say, without any preamble because this situation is too much to delay telling her and damn it, she should know.

Her brows furrow and she sets down her book to stare at me, so maybe some more explanation is needed.

"I did it to prove that while I continue to do the paperwork and severely be limited in my life outside this building because Dad and Junior can't handle it all, I thought you all needed proof I should be the one to take over. Well, Dad and Junior are trying to enter the same competition now, so I don't care whether this family gives this whole place to Junior to run into the ground anymore. I'm going to win this thing, and I'm done doing all the work by myself to keep this place going the way it should. I'm going to live my life and if this place goes to Junior, fine. I'll start my own restaurant."

Her mouth drops open and I walk away, out the front door and down to the parking lot. My phone is in my pocket with my wallet, Campbell is on his way, the saffron is in my hands, and I have work to do.

CHAPTER 29

*C*ampbell pulls into the lot just as I'm walking out of it; he stops the car and I get in.

"Please get me out of here," I say, and he looks concerned, but he does as I ask.

Now that I'm in his car, pulling away from the building that contains my whole life, not sure if it will continue to be that big of a deal to me, my hands start shaking.

"Olivia?" Campbell says. It isn't really a question, but it holds a million of them inside it.

"We need to go to Pike Place, and then stop by a shop on Mercer, but after that do you think we could finish the competition recipe at your house?" I ask, not answering any of his unspoken questions for a second while I try to still my hands and breathe.

"Uh, that's a great idea. My aunt will be happy to help, and we only have a week left," he says, finding a turn to take us in the direction we need to go and managing not to push me to answer him at this second.

His ability to always do what I need, does calm down the nerves racing through my body.

"Eight days," I say, "The competition is next Monday. And thank you." I lean across the seat to kiss him on the cheek and he takes my hand.

"Junior and my dad are trying to enter the competition too," I say, and his eyebrows shoot up. "For the same reason I want to, so Junior can add it to his list of reasons he should take over."

"Olivia, I know you love your dad, and I love you, but he's being terrible about this. If he gives the place to your brother, I might have to punch him," he says, shaking his head.

My heart skips a beat, and then another as I realize what he just blurted out.

I squeeze his hand, unable to suppress a giant smile, although I bite my lip to try. My shaking and anger are far behind me now.

"What did you just say?" I ask.

He looks over at me and quirks an eyebrow at the look on my face. I must be giving him whiplash with my emotional state right now, but I don't care and can't stop how I feel.

"You're smiling."

"Usually it's customary to smile when your boyfriend makes a declaration of love," I say, and his mouth pops open but no sound comes out.

"I..." His voice trails off and I see him going through the words in his head, playing back our conversation.

"So, when, exactly, did you decide you love me?" I ask. I'm sure it was just a general love like I would say about Deacon because I think he's great, but this is delicious to watch.

"Campbell, it's okay. I know you didn't mean it like that. But it's fun to hear anyway." I kiss him across the seat again, letting go of the saffron box to cup his cheek with my hand.

He relaxes under my fingers and I feel his half smile form under my fingers.

"You really are going to kill me," he says, and I laugh as I kiss his neck.

We get to Pike Place Market, driving around for a while before we find a spot to park.

"Okay, so what is the plan here?" he asks, taking my hand and walking with me into the cobblestoned street.

"First, we're going into the bakery there and getting breakfast," I say, pointing to one of my favorite places in the city. "And then we need to get the seafood. Everything else I can make with stuff from the grocery store after I figure out what is already at your house."

The aroma of freshly baked bread is leaking out the door and by the time we near it I'm getting drunk off the smell.

"Mmm, that is one of the best scents in the world," I say.

"One of," he says, pulling me into him and inhaling my neck.

"Not here." I pull myself away to a respectable distance, but I'm smiling and so is he.

The door opens as we approach, other patrons walking out as we go in. The display cases are full of delights, donuts, scones, muffins, so many breads, and what we came for.

"You should try the cinnamon rolls, that's what I'm getting. They're so good." I close my eyes and inhale, taking a minute to revel in the feeling this place fills me with. Few things aren't made better by good pastry or bread.

"Done," he says.

We loiter in the shop at one of two tiny tables, eating our cinnamon rolls. He makes noises that tell me I was right to suggest them.

"Have a good day," the lady behind the counter calls out as we head out the door.

"Thank you, you too," Campbell says.

He's so good in all the social situations. I don't know how he does it all the time. He seems to never say the wrong thing and he wins everyone over after they've spoken to him for five minutes. I do fine with limited contact, but it usually seems like the longer I'm around someone the less they like me. Maybe I can just watch and learn from him.

The traffic in the market, all on foot, is picking up. A winter day that's overcast and grey, but blessedly clear of rain, means that by noon this place will be crammed full of people.

We make our way to the fish sellers and carefully pick from the selections, asking about the freshest clams and calamari and I get a crab for the stock as well. After that, we drive to the grocery store and collect the other things I'll need.

My phone chimes in my pocket, letting me know I've timed our errand right and our next pickup is ready for us.

Once we're inside the car I check, and direct Campbell to the business he's never been to or heard of before.

"A sign maker?" Campbell asks as we head inside the office.

"Yep. You'll see." The man who runs the place has me sign for the box after I look inside and make sure everything looks right, it's all good and he'll just charge it to the business card I gave him this morning in our call.

Back in Luke Spacecruiser, I can barely contain how excited I am and turn to Campbell while I almost hop up and down.

"Show me, you're bouncing so this must be good," he says, smiling.

"Well, we've never had nametags before, and now we do," I say, handing him his and holding up my own.

His says his name and his pronouns, so does mine.

"Wait, what?" he asks, his half smile in full effect.

"They all have pronouns."

His smile falls, his face becomes blank and he reaches out for the box, looking through the nametags.

I think I screwed up.

But he pulls me to him, spilling the nametags off the seat of the car, and kisses me.

"Olivia," he says, hugging me tight as I squeeze him back.

We pull apart, smiling and collect the nametags back into the box, but he keeps his and tucks it into his jacket pocket.

My mind is back to the competition recipe by the time we get to his house, running over how I think it would be best to make it come to life and be not just good, but good enough to win.

CHAPTER 30

Carmen is sitting at the table drinking from a mug when we get inside the house with all of our ingredients.

"Good morning," she says, but her eyebrows are down and her voice suggests it isn't very good. "Campbell did you come home last night?"

He laughs, "Yes, Tia, I got in late, and we got an early start."

"What do you have there?" she asks, her eyebrows have evened out, but her voice still has a careful quality to it.

"I know it's probably a huge imposition, and I'm sorry, but we were wondering if we could work here on a new pizza I'm making for a competition." I lift the bags in my hands as Campbell moves into the kitchen to put his onto the counter.

She gets up from the table and meets me in the kitchen, so she can look through the bags.

"Ah, you went to get the fresh catch," she says, and finally smiles. "I was worried my nephew took advantage of you, *linda*."

He and I exchange a glance and I'm smiling as my cheeks flame in a blush.

"No, Tia, I am a gentleman," he says, and I bite my lip thinking about my invitation of the night before.

So, it wasn't just my dad's and my brother's reactions he was worried about. We have some old-fashioned ideas hanging on among our family members; I'm going to have to remember that.

"It's my fault, I called and woke him up kind of early even though we got in late," I say and focus on taking the ingredients out of the bags instead of whatever silent communication she's having with Campbell through their eyebrows.

"What is this new pizza?" she says, washing her hands in the sink and clearly preparing to help.

"It's paella pizza," I say, taking her place at the sink to wash my own hands. Campbell joins me, his side brushing mine, and my cheeks heat.

This might prove to be more difficult to get done than I thought if I can't focus on the cooking instead of him. I shake my head and remind myself of all that's riding on this recipe. There's a lot I need to accomplish with just a pizza. The place inside me where the cold anger comes from responds to my reminder of my mission and my brain sets Campbell into the role of assistant, not boyfriend, for right now.

"What do we need to do first?" he asks.

"The seafood stock and our house sauce needs to be made before we can make the combined sauce or the dough," I say, getting out the crab.

"I will make the stock. I don't know what your house sauce is," Carmen says, getting out a pot and starting on her task.

"Okay, Campbell, where are your spices?" I ask, rubbing my hands together.

"Are you sure you want to share Joe's famous sauce with us? Isn't it a secret?" he asks, smiling while he opens a cupboard filled with spices.

"Campbell, are you saying I shouldn't trust you?" I ask, shuffling through the well-stocked cupboard and collecting the things I need. I'm mostly kidding, I do trust them with the sauce recipe, but it's still hard to completely trust him as a boyfriend. My track record tells me I should be careful.

"Olivia," he says, that half smile on his face and his eyes soft. He touches my hand, taking spices from me, but lingering with our fingers touching.

"Ah, *amor joven*," Carmen says, shaking her head.

I only know a little Spanish, but *amor* is pretty obvious, and all my ability to block Campbell from distracting me flies away.

He coughs and steps back from me to put the spices on the counter next to the stove.

With Campbell chopping, Carmen and I at the stove, the sauces are well on their way to started and everything is prepped for the dough and the topping by the time Omar wanders out of his room in boxer shorts and no shirt with his hair sticking up all over his head.

I can't help laughing as he freezes when he spots us. Not that long ago I would have loved to be at his house in the morning and see him like this, now it's just funny.

"Omar," Carmen says, but she doesn't have to finish, he raises his hands.

"Uh, I'll go change. Sorry, Olivia," he says, and darts back down the hallway to his room.

"Did he really just apologize to me? I'm in your house unexpectedly." I go back to cooking, shaking my head, and miss how Campbell doesn't answer.

CHAPTER 31

"What's next?" Carmen asks hours later after the sauce is combined and bubbling, the clams and calamari are ready, and the dough is prepped. She's been engrossed in every step of the process.

"Now we spread the sauce on the dough," I say, taking the ladle out of the sauce and going about my task, getting the coating perfect and even the first time because I've been doing this my whole life. Whatever muscle memory I have, it's probably all things like this. Cooking. Pizza.

"And then we put on the cheese," I say, sprinkling the cheese in a thick layer. "Last, we put these on." The calamari and the clams I sprinkle on top of it all.

"The only thing left to do now is pop it all in the oven." In it goes, and I set the timer.

"More work goes into a pizza than I thought. It isn't something I make," Carmen says, standing back and looking at me with her head cocked to the side.

She's evaluating me again, and the heat creeps up my neck in response.

Campbell passes me a glass of lemonade and I down it in two gulps, not just because it helps cool my cheeks, but because I haven't stopped to drink anything since we started and it's been hours now.

"Thank you," I say when I'm done, and his eyebrows are high with his mouth in the half smile.

"Maybe next time you do a marathon cooking session I should just be standing by with a drink with a straw to shove in your face," he says and laughs.

I smile at him. He has a point.

"You have been working in your restaurant all your life. Have you done much other cooking besides pizza?" Carmen asks and my smile fades.

Campbell is cleaning up the messy bits we've left in the kitchen and I join him to keep my hands busy.

"No. I wish we had a menu of more things, but focusing on pizza makes more business sense my dad says." Which I understand, looking at how much we would have to add to the orders from our suppliers to branch out at all.

"What about cooking in your home? Have you done much of that?" Carmen asks, still in the same position as before. It makes me think she's trying to figure something out, but I don't know what.

"No. We actually don't do a lot of cooking at home. I have cooked some things for myself, but making anything in single servings is kind of hard." I stop myself from adding more, the urge to ramble on about how I enjoy making bread because the pressure of her gaze is getting to me so much it's almost overwhelming. But nothing good comes from me rambling.

"You know your way around a kitchen and clearly enjoy it, but when we made empanadas together you were," she says, her hand waving in the air. It looks like she's searching for the right word to say. "It was bliss for you, that time discovering new things in the kitchen. Today it seems like a job, a mission. I do not understand it, *linda*."

"I…" There are not words to answer her. I don't know what to say.

"Olivia loves her family restaurant; she wants to take it over some day," Campbell says, taking my hand.

"When is whatever that great smell is going to be done? I'm starving," Omar says, walking into the kitchen, wearing clothes this time, and I've never been happier to see him.

"Are you going to be a taster then?" I ask, wiping down the last section of counter, returning the kitchen to the state it was in when we took it over this morning.

"You should probably tell me what we're tasting," Omar takes a seat at the island.

"Let's leave it a surprise and see what he thinks when he tastes it," Campbell says.

"That's a good idea. Omar, if you taste what I think you will, I'll know I'm a success," I say. My smile is huge because I'm sure he's going to know this is a paella pizza, it's just too good.

"It will tell us if the pizza is a success," Campbell says, giving my hand a squeeze.

"That's what I said." I frown at him and the timer goes off on the pizza. Carmen's oven mitt is cobalt blue with the Mariner's logo on it; it works, but it's weird to pull the pizza out by any means other than with the big board from the restaurant.

Paella, when done right, looks like a bunch of things thrown together, not like a carefully arranged display on a plate in some Michelin restaurant. My pizza has a similar look to the original dish, but is more like a Monet, there is an order to this chaos. It's exactly how I want it to look.

The smell wafting off of it is so similar to Paella that I can't help but squeal a little.

"Olivia, that looks amazing," Campbell says.

"Smells even better," Omar says, a huge smile on his face and he looks like he's almost drooling.

"It's good so far." Is all I'll allow myself to say out loud. I don't want to risk jinxing it.

Carmen helps me cut the pizza and plate it for each of us.

I stare at them as they take their first bites. Campbell shuts his eyes, Omar mmm's, Carmen takes a small bite, considering it as she chews, and then she nods her head and takes another bite.

Finally, I take a bite, ensuring I get a piece of all the ingredients in one taste.

Paella pizza is a success. The flavor in my mouth is very reminiscent of the dish that inspired it, but with Dad's sauce added in, the dough of the crust, and the cheese, it is unmistakably a pizza still. I love it.

"Well, Omar, you're the only one who doesn't know what this pizza is called, what do you think it would be called?" I ask and take another bite.

"It's really good, but it reminds me of something that isn't pizza. Is there saffron in this?" he asks, instead of answering.

"Good find. Yes, there is," Campbell says.

Come on, Omar, please know what this is.

"It's almost like paella," he says, and I try not to choke on the bite in my mouth while I whoop.

"Did I guess right?" he asks and laughs while Campbell pounds on my back.

My eyes are watering from choking, but I've never been happier to have a piece of food lodged in my throat. All my worry about the restaurant going to Junior, all my work for this to be a successful recipe is paying off.

CHAPTER 32

Campbell and I spend the rest of the day together, mostly in the basement of his house. We watch movies, he tries, and fails, to teach me how to be as good as he is at pool, and we kiss. A lot.

When it's getting close to dinner time, and the time I should probably be heading home, we're on the couch watching another movie, and I realize we have been spending all of our time working toward my goals, and I don't know his.

"Campbell," I say, turning my face to his from where I'm tucked under his arm, "what do you want to do?"

He looks at me, his fingers running along my arm, and gives me his half smile, this one full of inuendo.

"Not that," I say, and the heat blooms up my neck. "I mean, I want to take over the restaurant, but what do you want to do?"

"Oh." He shifts, sitting up a little straighter. "I'm not sure. There's no money for college after everything." He gestures at himself and I realize I never thought about how much it costs just to be him. "Part of the reason I agreed to come here was because my mom couldn't afford the tuition for the

International School at home anymore and Washington has the free online high school here."

"I'm not sorry you're here, but I'm sorry you had to leave your home. It must suck to miss your senior year with your friends," I say, entwining my fingers into his.

"Thank you, but I think it worked out good for me," he says, and kisses me.

His kisses make all my worries about work float away, all the calm he brings me just by being around works to block all the distractions outside of he and I, but they make my physical response to him worse. My heart picks up its pace and my stomach floats away as he kisses me.

When he stops, he smiles at me and I realize he hasn't answered the question.

"You can't avoid answering me forever, no matter how much I like kissing you."

"Maybe that's my plan though. Just keep kissing you." He buries his face in my neck and starts kissing it.

I groan and have to untangle our legs and physically push myself away from him far enough that he can't get to me for a minute. As I move down the couch he leans after me, I let him fall on his face on the cushion that's now between us and laugh as he growls into it.

"Are you going to survive?" I ask, giggling at him as he shakes his head, still face down on the couch.

"Poor Campbell." I make a pouty face and he finally looks up at me and grins.

"Olivia, you really are going to kill me." He sits up and looks at his hands.

"For a long time, there were things I worked toward, things I thought I would do like playing pool. But some of those things are out of the realm of possibility for me now. I had to choose between who I am and my plans. So, my dear, persistent, won't just kiss me, Olivia, the answer is, I don't know."

His voice isn't angry, or even sad, it's resigned. He's clearly had to go through this in his head for too long for it to be as painful as it really is. Like a word said over and over loses its meaning, the loss of the plans he had for his life in order to live as himself has lost the edge it once had for him. But nothing has blunted the pain I feel for him.

Tears are dripping off my chin onto my hands before I realize I'm crying.

"Campbell, you deserve all the things you've ever wanted. I want to help you get as many of them as I possibly can," I say, my voice is hard. Like I'm daring the unfair universe to contradict me.

He looks up at me and his face melts into the soft half smile he wore while we were dancing at Katie and Deacon's birthday party. He scoots across the couch to me and I don't stop him as he kisses me this time.

"You are what I want now," he says, his forehead to mine and my heart dancing in joy.

"If you could do anything in the world, if the world didn't suck, what would you do?" I ask, my fingers playing with the hair at the nape of his neck.

"Play pool and write books," he says with a sigh, like admitting his dreams out loud costs him something. Maybe it does and I'm a jerk for pushing.

"You know, you can absolutely still write books, and you don't have to get a Master's in Fine Arts to do it." I kiss his nose and look at him, trying to convince him with my eyes alone that his dreams aren't dead. They might be changed, but they aren't dead.

"Maybe I could find a way to pay the bills and write books at the same time. I worry about finding the balance needed to do that, but I can try," he says, he doesn't sound sure, but I'll keep reminding him.

"And you can still school the whole state in pool anytime there's a game." I'm rewarded with a small laugh.

"From now on, I'll just hold your dreams out for you to look at from time to time so you don't forget them. You helped me with mine, and this is me helping you with yours."

*H*e drops me off at home; we linger in the parking lot for more kisses before I hop out of his car, wave, and head up the stairs.

Walking by the restaurant floor, I can hear the muffled noise from within all the way out here. The Sunday dinner crowd is a noisy one tonight. The Seahawks must have won the game today.

Our front door holds silence on the other side of it. Opening the door, I'm met with a house without any lights on. That's weird. Mom usually turns on some lights, unless she's having a migraine. I run to the living room and she isn't on the couch. Sprinting to her bedroom, the door is cracked and there's no glow from the TV spilling out so I slow because she must be having a bad headache and the last thing I want to do is disturb her with my footsteps. I have to check on her though, make sure she doesn't need anything.

Pushing open her door a little more, squinting into the dark, I find my mom. Laying on the floor on her stomach, one hand sprawled out.

"Mom," I cry and dart to her side, throwing the door all the way open, the faint light of the moon through the window the only illumination in the room.

Her pulse is steady in her neck when I check, and bending down, she's breathing fine, but she doesn't answer me when I call her name.

I pull my phone out of my pocket and call down to the restaurant, Junior picks up.

"Joe's pizzeria, how may I help you?" he says, the background noise of people doing the Sea, and others following with Hawks almost too loud to understand him.

"Junior, tell Dad. Mom's unconscious. I'm calling an ambulance." I end the call and dial 911. He'll know what to do.

When the operator picks up, I tell her our address, making sure to let her know we are up the back stairs not in the restaurant, and explain what's going on, including Mom's cancer.

"Mommy, just hold on. Help is coming," I whisper into her ear, hoping she hears me.

Dad slams into the door as he rushes into the room and then drops to the floor beside Mom. He checks the same signs I did and tells her to hang on and that he loves her.

My hands are shaking, but I lace the fingers of her thrown out hand in mine and shove my nerves down. I can fall apart later, right now Mom and Dad both need me calm. He's crying, the tears flowing down his cheeks and he makes no effort to wipe them away.

It feels like it takes forever for the ambulance to arrive, I watch every single time Mom's chest rises and falls the entire time, but when I check my phone, it's been less than four minutes.

The paramedics come in the door with all their equipment and I jump up to give them room and turn on the light.

Mom groans when the light comes on and I can't stop the

sob from bursting out of me. I press my fist to my mouth and choke down the tears as the paramedics load her onto a board and carry her out, Dad following them as I trail behind.

When the front door shuts, I collapse to the floor, bury my face in my hands and cry wracking, wretched sobs.

CHAPTER 34

My phone chimes in my pocket, telling me I have a text. Through blurry eyes I see Campbell has messaged me.

I'm working tomorrow, are you? Will I see you?

I text him back, my fingers shaking the whole time and relying on autocorrect for some of the words because I can't key things in right through my tears.

Mom is going to hospital. Found her collapsed.

I call the restaurant again because Junior should know what's going on and get away as soon as he can.

He answers on the first ring, I imagine him standing beside it waiting for word.

"Junior," I say, and break down again.

"Oh, god. Olivia, is she…" He chokes on the other end of the line.

"No. She's breathing, was when I came in. But she collapsed and has been laying on her stomach on the floor in the dark for who knows how long. She didn't talk, but she groaned when the lights came on. I should have been here," I say, my voice thick and barely intelligible through my tears.

"It isn't your fault. I'm glad you found her. I…" He trails of and take a series of deep, ragged breaths. "I should go and take care of this place. She's in good hands now."

He hangs up and I drop my phone, curling into a ball on the floor.

All the possibilities of what this could mean, that she's getting worse, that she was really hurt from a simple trip and fall because of her nerve damage, or that she has secondary infection which is so dangerous for her right now, run through my head on a loop. They don't stay away even as I banish them one by one, the next coming right behind the first to slam into me in fresh waves of fear for my mother.

Mom was the life of the party, a social butterfly, and so damn strong before she got sick. I have to remind myself of those sides of her now, it's been so long since she was herself.

The front door creaks open again and in the dark of the hall I don't know who is coming toward me, nor do I care. The only light is spilling into the room from my parent's bedroom and it isn't enough to see through my tears.

Campbell scoops me onto his lap, wrapping his arms around me and I wail in a fresh wave of tears.

"Shh, I've got you. Olivia, I've got you."

CHAPTER 35

*E*ventually the tears run out and Campbell takes me and Junior to the hospital; by the time we get there, Mom is admitted and we have ten minutes to visit her.

"I'll stay in the waiting room," Campbell says.

I want to argue, to drag him with me so he can hold me up if I can't do it on my own.

He must see the panic rising on my face because he wraps me into his arms, his voice in my ear as he says, "It's okay, Olivia. I'm right here, and you can do this." He kisses me on the forehead, and I turn to follow Junior down the hall.

A hospital hallway is a strange place, and one I've become too accustomed to over the last two years of Mom's illness. Today I can't ignore the machines narrowing the over wide space, or that it has to be so wide in case they need to move a bed through it. I can't ignore the hurried steps of the nurses, or the stacks of paperwork crowding the huge circular desk. All of it, from the ugly pale green of the walls to the stringent smell of the disinfectant tickling my nose, makes me wonder if it will be needed for my mom and if it is needed for her, will she come home?

Mom is awake and sitting up in the bed when we get to her. Junior picks up speed; he would be running if there was more space between Mom and the door, but I freeze, loitering in the doorway.

Tears are threatening at the back of my eyes, weighty and putting pressure on my fuzzy brain. My mom is awake, for now. But what happened?

"Junior, I'm okay," she says, but she isn't. Her skin is a sickly greige, none of the healthy pink tinge I'm used to. Her wrist is in a cast, and her fingers on Junior's back look like her bones are wearing a skin suit, there is nothing to them.

"What happened?" he asks, and I realize my hands are shaking.

"My stupid legs gave out and I fell. I guess I went down wrong and broke my wrist and my body decided I should pass out until someone was there to help," she says, looking past him to me and smiling.

I'm wringing my hands together to stop their shaking and Mom's desiccated hand waves me toward her.

"Thank you, Olivia. You did wonderfully, you did everything right." Her voice is thready, without any of the power she usually has.

She reaches her hand in the cast out to me and I fold it into my own, bending so my forehead is touching the rough plaster of her cast. Her other hand rests on the top of my head and the tears fall onto our entwined fingers.

Our family can't lose her. I can't lose her. I need my mother; we all do.

"Listen, Junior," Dad says, his voice scratchy like he's been screaming. "Your sister has school so I need you to take up some more work at the restaurant, and Olivia, I'm sorry, but you're going to have to work more too. I need to be here with your Mom until she can come home. They want to do some tests and I won't leave her until she can come home."

Pulling myself away from my mother's hand, I sit up and nod, Junior nodding beside me. Whatever our current issues, right now, this moment, requires us to get our ingredients in order and focus or we won't get this recipe right, and this recipe is everything.

"I love you kids. Junior, Olivia, you know that, right? I'll be home soon," Mom says; her smile is brittle, but she smiles anyway.

"I love you too," Junior says, leaning in to kiss Mom on the cheek before he stands up.

"Dad," I say, looking across Mom to my bedraggled father, "I'll bring a bag of stuff for you both. I'll pack as soon as we get home." I get up and move to be near Mom's head, to lean into her and kiss her wax paper thin cheek. "I love you."

Junior and I leave her room as a nurse is stepping inside to usher us out. I wipe the tears from my eyes and start scheduling my world, focusing on the practical, on the things I need to do so I can make it through whatever this new reality is.

Campbell stands up from a waiting room chair when we get to him, his arm encircling me immediately. I tuck my face into his neck and inhale peaches that can't entirely remove the disinfectant from my nose.

"She's okay. She broke her wrist," I say into his neck and he squeezes me tighter.

"Dad's staying here tonight," Junior says, "but Olivia and I need to get a bag packed for them and I'll bring it back here."

I unfurl myself from Campbell, who's nodding to Junior, and reach out to touch my brother's hand.

"Let's go," he says, squeezing my hand.

CHAPTER 36

After Junior and I pack their things, Junior heads back to the hospital to drop them off and Campbell is waiting for me in our living room.

"Do you have to go home?" I ask, hugging my arms around myself preparing for him to say that yes, he's leaving me.

"No, I called Carmen and let her know what's going on and she said if you need me to stay," he says and I launch myself into his arms, the first weak smile I've had since walking in the door playing on my mouth. "She also said that if I don't act honorably, she'll skin me and use me to make empanadas."

I manage a small laugh, more thankful than I can express for Carmen and for Campbell.

"Good," I say, taking his hand and leading him to my room.

Walking in the door to my turret bedroom, I'm struck by how it must look to him. My old rug is still rolled up in the corner and my walls are painfully sparse. The only thing that holds any sign of life beyond the colors of the bedding and the rug is my desk, with stacks of papers and files from the restaurant.

He looks around, taking it all in, but not commenting.

"It's kind of sad how little life I still have in here, huh?" I ask, watching carefully as half his mouth quirks up.

"Well, I like it. When did you get the new rug?" he asks, looking at the one rolled up and listing in the corner.

"Believe it or not," I say, and cough trying to decide if this is a good thing to admit to him, "I still had the stuff in here from when I was ten, but I ordered the one you're standing on and the bedding right after we met."

"It's nice." His voice is soft, and I wonder if he sees what I see, his eyes have taken over my whole world.

"Stay here. I'll get you some pajamas pants and go change." I let go of his hand and take a sleep shirt from a drawer before I head to Junior's room to steal a pair of pajamas. In the doorway of my room I toss the pants to Campbell and go to the bathroom to change.

Whatever Carmen worries will be going on tonight, I just want to snuggle up next to my boyfriend and know I'm not alone so I can sleep.

I knock on the door before I walk into my room. "Are you ready?"

"Yes," he says on the other side.

He's folding his discarded clothes onto the chair at my desk and is waiting for me in a white t-shirt and my brother's pajama pants which hang too low and too lose on his hips.

When he looks up at me as I walk in, he drops the carefully folded pants he's holding in a heap and his mouth drops open.

"Are…" I swallow and tug on the tattered white sleep shirt where it hits me mid-thigh before I try again. "Are you okay?"

He drags a hand across his face and smiles that half smile at me, one eyebrow lifting.

"You really are going to kill me. It's okay, I can handle it. Come here," he says, reaching a hand out for me.

I go to him and take his hand, leading him to my bed, switching off the light on the way. We climb into my bed and I tuck my head under his chin, resting it on his chest.

"Why did you say I'm going to kill you? This is not exactly an amazing outfit," I say as he plays with my hair.

He clears his throat and waits until I'm not sure he's going to answer me.

"The t-shirts," he says, and it leaves me still not understanding why my old over-sized t-shirts always trigger such a strong response from him. "I have a thing about a girl in a long t-shirt with white socks."

I can't help it, I'm laughing. I feel bad to laugh on a night when my mother is in the hospital and I don't want to make him feel weird, but it's so random and I'm laughing until my eyes water.

"Oh, thanks, Olivia," he says, but he's laughing too.

And then we're kissing, his hands in my hair and mine clinging to him like he's the rope that will pull me in from drowning. He kisses me until I'm breathless and then tucks me back into my position on his chest so we can sleep.

In the morning, when my alarm goes off, I wake up in the same position, which I never do. Campbell's calming influence while I'm awake seems to let me sleep the same way, as calm as possible.

"Hey," he says, after I reach across him to turn off the alarm clock's wailing.

"Good morning," I say into his chest before I give him a quick peck and scramble from the bed.

"What's the matter?" he asks, sitting up.

"I don't want you to smell my morning breath," I blurt, and he smiles as I dart into the bathroom. I hear him moving around in my room while I brush my teeth and run a brush through my hair. I can't do anything about the dark circles under my eyes, but at least my breath doesn't smell when I walk back out again as he pulls his sweater over his head. He's already back into his jeans.

"You need to go to school today?" he asks, smiling at me and making it a point to smack a stick of gum in his mouth.

I pull his face to mine and kiss him, tasting the freshness of his gum.

"Unfortunately," I say.

"How about I drive you to school before I head home and get ready for my shift?" He tucks a wayward strand of my hair behind an ear and his hand lingers on the side of my face.

"Perfect."

CHAPTER 37

By the time lunch rolls around, I'm dragging, Campbell isn't here, and all my worries for my mom are hanging onto my back, trailing me down the hallways.

When I get to my table full of my friends Deacon and Katie stop their conversation to cock their heads at me, their brows furrowed.

"Are you okay, Olivia?" Katie asks.

"She and Campbell had a long night," Omar says; it takes me a second to remember that he would know because Campbell lives with him.

"Oh, really?" Katie says, her eyebrows wiggling in innuendo.

"Damn," Deacon says. "Olivia, you're going to have to go easy on my man, he's already madly in love with you. If you break his heart after this I'm going to have to choose, and I don't want to." He takes a huge bite of his hamburger and shakes his head.

"You guys, nothing happened. My mom went to the hospital, so Campbell took care of me. We slept. That's all," I say, and my face floods with heat.

"Your mom?" Katie asks, wearing the same expression of immediate shift to concern that her cousin does.

"She," I start and have to look down at my food, away from them. I don't like talking about this. The last thing I want is for my friends to remind me to contemplate the worst case scenario and it always seems to happen when people learn of her diagnosis, the questions everyone has afterward. I clear my throat and try again. "She has cancer."

"Oh, Livvy, I'm sorry." Deacon's voice is a low rumble and it reminds me of my dad.

"Is she like you?" Katie asks and I snap my eyes up to look at her, not sure what she means or how it could be relevant what my mother and I have in common.

"Yes," Theresa says, coming to sit by me and putting a hand on my shoulder. "So, she's going to beat it."

She's the only one of my friends that knows my mom, and her words make me bite my lip to stop the tears in my eyes from falling.

"Well, of course you didn't do anything last night then," Katie says. "I was going to give you hell for not getting on that when you had the chance, but I get it." Katie's voice is so full of remorse and sincerity, it makes me smile.

"Helping you through an emergency, that's even worse," Deacon says. "The pining."

Katie sweeps the back of her hand to her forehead and wilts into Deacon's side.

"Oh, Campbell, I need you," she says.

"Katie, shut up," I say, but I'm laughing. On a terrible day, after a worse night, I'm laughing.

"So, nothing happened?" she asks, leaning across the table.

"Um," I say, putting another French fry in my mouth so I don't have to answer.

"Good, grief, Katie. Omar needs to spend more time with

you so you can stop being so desperate for details," Theresa says, taking a bite of her own burger and smiling around the bite.

She looks guilty as hell, and it reminds me that not so long ago it would have been details about Theresa and me Katie would have been mining for. But would Theresa have been there for me when my mother fell? As careful as she always was about hiding our relationship, I doubt it.

I smile, thinking about Campbell and how good he is to me.

"You're smiling. Something totally happened. Alright, I'm happy now," Katie says, sitting back in her seat and taking a bite of her lunch, a smug grin on her face.

"Baby, you make no sense," Omar says, kissing Katie's cheek and shaking his head.

"Nope. But you love me anyway," she says, kissing his cheek back.

They're good together, I decide, while I eat my lunch and watch these people I barely knew a couple months ago. I'm glad it's working out the way it is.

"So, when is that competition?" Omar asks me a little later.

"What competition?" Deacon asks, sitting up straighter.

It makes me think about what a monster he is on the football field and how, as pure as he is, he's got a competitive streak.

"A week from today I'm in a pizza competition. I'll be missing school next Monday so I can get ready for it," I say.

"Will there be tasting involved?" Deacon asks, leaning toward me.

"The way to your heart really is through food," I say, and everyone laughs. "After the judges sample, then I suppose."

"How do I get to be a judge of something like that? That's a dream job," Deacon says and sighs.

"Most of the time they're famous chefs or food critics," I say, and I see the wheels turning in his head, it makes me smile.

"Are you going to use our house to cook again?" Omar asks, and Deacon shoots us a dirty look.

"You cooked at his house and I wasn't invited?" Deacon looks genuinely hurt, his mouth hanging open in a pout.

"I'm sorry. I should have called you," I say; he humphs in response.

"Omar, do you think your mom would let me do that? I don't know what your schedules are all like," I say.

"Probably. You can come by after school and ask her. She loves you so any time she can spend with you I'm sure she would like, and I don't know her schedule either. Nurses have weird schedules," he says.

I put some of my fries on Deacon's plate as a peace offering and he grins at me before popping one into his mouth. It reminds me of the amazing yucca fries Carmen made.

"Hey, Omar, do you think your mom would be okay with me adding her yucca fries to the menu at the restaurant and calling them Carmen fries?" I ask, he puts down his burger and furrows his brow.

"Really? You think they would sell at a pizza place?" he asks.

"It can't hurt to try. I could give her a cut of the profits," I say, thinking out how I would tag the sales of them in the point of sale software so I could do that.

"That's a cool idea. And Olivia, thanks for not just stealing the recipe," Omar says, and Katie and Deacon nod.

"Would you be mad if I straight up stole it to make for myself at home?" I ask and they all laugh.

CHAPTER 38

At the end of the school day, I need to make my trip to see Carmen quick so I can get to work. I can't wait to see Campbell, and by now I'm sure the restaurant needs me. Omar and I walk to his house together from school and I wonder that I ever had a thing for him.

He's still perfect Omar, still adorable, and I'm happy he's with Katie, but nothing happens when I look at him. My heart doesn't dance the salsa and my stomach stays asleep. He looks like his cousin, but Campbell, before and after the sharpening of his jaw and the shading of more stubble growing in, is breath stealing beautiful to me. Campbell is the perfect recipe in all his forms, the kind you know is going to be good even while you're putting it together before it's all the way cooked.

"Omar, why did you thank me for not stealing the recipe for the restaurant if you don't mind me making it at home?" I ask, interrupting his five minute long rant about football.

"Oh, well, it's about cultural appropriation," he says.

We step around a mother with her baby in a stroller, giving her room on the sidewalk.

"How is it different when I make it at home, then?" I truly don't understand how to do it right, how to be respectful.

"It's about the profiting off of it. If you did a pizza inspired by the flavors of empanadas or something, I think it would be different, because you're making a whole new thing. But exactly the same recipe, it's cool to make for yourself, I mean I hope everyone makes Dominican food for themselves because it's the best. But profiting off someone else's work without giving credit is kind of shitty."

"Huh, okay. That makes sense," I say, thinking about how much of food mixes together flavors all over the world, and how I'll have to be mindful when I take over the restaurant.

"Campbell's at work, sorry," Omar says as we walk up his driveway.

"I know, it's okay. I'll see him in a bit. I can't stay long; I have to work too."

The steps to his front door have salt sprinkled on them to stave off the ice from forming that is starting to coat everything in the city at night as the fog and freezing temperatures roll in.

"Mom, I'm home, and I brought Olivia," Omar calls as we go into the living room.

Carmen comes in from the hall to the bedrooms in scrubs.

"Omar, *linda*, what are you two doing here?" Carmen asks, kissing her son on the cheek and smiling at me.

"I hope it isn't an imposition, but I wanted to ask if I could use your kitchen again next Monday to prep for the competition," I say, taking my backpack off my shoulders to give them a rest, and setting it on the floor.

"Of course, it will be nice to say the winning pizza was made in my kitchen," she says, going into the kitchen to pour herself a cup of coffee.

"How is your mother?" she asks, her face full of concern that reminds me of my mom and I have to swallow to stay upbeat enough to answer.

"She's doing all right. Thank you for letting Campbell stay with me. It was bad enough, but without someone I love there to help me through it, I don't know," I say, shaking my head.

Omar whoops, and I spin to look at him, his reaction so not right at the moment.

"You love Campbell," he says, and I open my mouth to argue, only to shut it again.

I clap my hands over my mouth and tears start pouring from my eyes while my face is immediately on fire, my blush must me tomato sauce red.

"Oh my god," I say, laughing.

"I'm so happy for you," Omar says, grabbing me in a hug.

Carmen is behind me clapping.

"Yes, yes," I say, stammering it over and over again as I realize that I do.

Omar hugs me again and kisses me on the cheek.

I bury my face in his chest and laugh at myself. A slip of the tongue and it feels like things have shifted. Now, I have to go to work and face Campbell with this knowledge in my head.

The front door slams and I pull back from Omar, his arms dropping from my sides.

"Who's here?" Carmen asks, going to the window, Omar and I in her wake.

Outside, Campbell stalks to his car wearing one shoe, the other is in his hand. He hurls his shoe into the car and takes off down the road.

"What's wrong with his shoe?" I ask, but neither of them answer me. None of us know what just happened.

Carmen and Omar assure me Campbell will be fine, they'll call him so I can go back to work. I text him on my walk over anyway, but he doesn't answer. He's probably driving.

At work, he isn't there, and we are slow which is a small favor because his absence leaves us short handed. After I've locked the front door and started cleaning up, Campbell walks in the back door wearing different shoes.

"Hey, what happened? Where've you been?" I ask, going to him, but he grabs my outstretched arms by the wrists and holds me at arm's length.

"I tripped and one of my shoes was basically destroyed. But I'm not coming back here. I know I should give my two weeks notice, but I don't care," he says, dropping my arms and stepping back from me. His face is hard, lips pursed, and his half smile looks like a sneer.

"Why aren't you coming back?" I ask, my hands are shaking, tears are threatening, and I might vomit. His words are heavy in my stomach, the look on his face telling me whatever he says next is going to break my heart.

"You played me, Olivia. I should have known. How could I be good enough for you and all your damn plans? We're done. You want someone I'm never going to be." He turns and stalks toward the door.

"Wai-" I choke on my words; my voice gives out on me. I have no idea what happened, but my cheeks are on fire, my whole body is trembling, and I can't look at him as he walks out the door. I stare at the floor instead and hug my shaking arms around my body while my tears drop onto the black and white tile floor.

CHAPTER 39

I mop, sweep, restock, wipe down, and count out. I do it all while choking on tears and barely able to hold onto the money because my hands are shaking so bad. Then I go into the office and email the principal from Dad's business account. I explain about Mom's diagnosis, and her being in the hospital, I ask for the principal to excuse me from school for a while and sign it from my father.

The schedule for the restaurant shifts is hanging on the wall where it always does, I tear it down and write my name into all of Campbell's, scratching his out with a thick black marker. My tears keep falling on the schedule and blurring the ink.

When I tore the paper off the wall, it ripped a chunk out of the top and I curse myself while I tape it back up. It's no longer pretty, or orderly, and I want to make a mess out of the whole office, take things from the desk and throw them against the walls. I don't. Of course, I don't.

My walk up the steps into our apartment is done in the dark, I don't bother to turn on the lights anywhere along the way, preferring to not face anything until I have to.

This morning, was it only this morning? This morning I thought the only thing wrong with my little corner of the world was my mother's illness. Now it feels like it's all falling down around me, every single ingredient is wrong, and I've burnt it all anyway.

In my room I collapse onto the bed, chucking the pillow my face falls into the second I realize it's the green one. At least I didn't see it in the dark. I climb into my covers, not bothering to take off my clothes. But the pillow smells like peaches. My tears wetting the fabric only make the smell grow stronger, it's the aroma that follows me into my dreams.

My dreams are nightmares of trying to find someone, I don't know who, while I run, tripping and falling, getting scratched by tree limbs, through a peach orchard. Each of the trees are heavy with fragrant fruit and as I pass them, they fall to the ground.

I wake before my alarm goes off. My back and hairline are clammy, my shirt is sodden. My flailing hand hits the alarm and turns it off. Part of me wishes I could go back to sleep, but I don't want to have nightmares again, and I can't lay around. I need to move, to do something, to get away in my mind by focusing on anything other than the last two days.

Getting ready is a slog because nothing of my morning routine takes away my mind's ability to dwell. Showering? Nope, it feels like all the time in the world to wonder how it went so wrong so fast. Getting dressed? Nope, staring at my sock drawer I realize I have a lot of white socks, and I don't want to wear them. Even brushing my hair makes me think of his hands running through it.

Walking through the living room, I trail my fingers along the blanket Mom has been using when she sits on the couch. It helps me prepare for facing the restaurant without Campbell to help me; my mom is facing so much more than I am. I can do this.

But stepping off the last step into the restaurant still knocks into me with a physical force, I hold my hand to my chest while I get an apron and start the prep. I spend all day sequestering myself in the kitchen, trying not to put on my shiny, happy customer face and be in the front of the house. But in the afternoon, my normal shift, I have no choice.

Fake it till you make it becomes a back of my brain echo. So, I'm standing at the till entering a bill, mumbling it to myself, when Katie rushes in the front door. Her arrival, for all her hurry, stops me in mid motion. I forget to say the words getting me through the day.

She swings her head around, looking through the dining room. When she's facing me, her shoulders rise and fall, her whole body relaxing before she smiles and makes her way to me.

"Olivia, thank god. I called you so many times. Are you okay? Is your mom okay?" Katie asks, reaching her hand out to touch mine where it hovers above the open register.

"I…" I start, and Deacon rattles the door in the frame as he barrels inside. He rubs a hand over his face and joins us at the register.

"We've been wrecks all day worrying about you; is everything okay? Why did you miss school?" he asks.

"Hi, guys. Um, my mom is the same. I just need to take some time off of school so I can cover here. We're short staffed," I say, not looking at them and pretending that finishing up this bill takes a hell of a lot more concentration than it does. But I feel my stupid, stupid face start to heat with a blush.

"Call Campbell in; I'm sure he'll pick up extra shifts to help. You shouldn't have to miss school." Katie relaxes into the counter and scans the room like she's looking for him.

"He—um." I cough, covering my mouth and trying again while my empty stomach grows heavy. "He quit."

Katie whips her head around to look at me, her nose scrunched up like she smells something bad, or maybe doesn't believe me.

"That doesn't make any sense. Why would he quit when he gets to see you all the time?" she asks and Deacon cocks his head to the side waiting for me to say out loud what I don't want to.

"He broke up with me," I say, my voice quavering and weak.

"But he is batshit crazy about you," Deacon says, his eyes huge.

Katie has her hands over her open mouth and a new worry blooms from their response, will they stick with me as a friend without Campbell around? He got me these friends, introduced us, will he get them in the split?

"I don't know why he did it. I wish he didn't, but he won't talk to me about it either. Maybe it was all too much for him, helping me win my place here, supporting me while my mom is in the hospital. I don't know." I need to go, to get out of this conversation, but I'm not sure how to do that and keep these relationships intact. I need my friends, but I don't know how to do that either. Maybe that's why he broke up with me.

"Guys, I need to get to work, can we talk about this later?" I ask, hoping blaming work will give me a pass.

"Okay, but we're getting a table and in between stuff keep coming by, we're going to figure this out," Katie says, squeezing my hand before turning to pull Deacon with her to a table.

After I grab them the drinks I know they'll want, I handle as many other tasks as possible until I head back to their table when there is nothing else for me to do. My plan to delay backfires. As soon as I sit down next to Katie, Omar comes through the door and heads our way.

He looks a little too much like his cousin for me at the moment and I turn in my seat to look at Katie, trying to choke down the tears threatening the backs of my eyes.

"Hey," Omar says, dropping into the seat next to Deacon.

"What did you find out?" Katie asks, leaning toward him.

"Campbell won't talk to me. The only thing he said is he needs time to be happy for me. Which, what the hell that means, he won't say," Omar says, taking Katie's hand across the table.

"I think it's probably this," Deacon says, gesturing to their entwined hands. "He just broke up with his girlfriend; he must mean he can't handle being around you with yours right now."

"Maybe," Katie says, biting her bottom lip.

"None of it makes sense though. He loves Olivia, and she loves him. It's all he's ever really wanted, for someone to love him as he really is, for him to be enough for someone. People at home said some ugly things when he came out," Omar says, shaking his head.

The tears fall, and I can't stop them.

"He told me he was never going to be enough for me because of all my plans. The other day I asked him what he wanted to do after he graduated, what his plans are. This is my fault. That's not what I meant." My voice cracks and I bury my face in my hands, my tears flowing through my fingers.

"That would be the stupidest reason ever to run from the person you love," Deacon says.

"Campbell isn't stupid," I say, lifting my head and wanting to punch my giant friend.

"No, he's not. So, this is extra bad; he's scared so he's running." Deacon pokes the table with his finger, his eyes narrowed.

"But this doesn't help. We need to figure out how Olivia can convince him; we should all help fix this. They're our friends and this is going to get really awkward, really fast." Katie's voice is hard, her eyes daring Omar and Deacon to contradict her.

"You guys can't help this. I have to figure it out. Like I know I can't use your kitchen to make the pizza on Monday, Omar," I say, trying and failing at making a joke. I wipe the tears off my face and get up.

"Listen, I appreciate you all wanting to help. I wish you could, but I have to make it through this on my own. And I have to get back to work. I'll see you."

Turning and walking away from my friends while they stare, their faces full of pity, sucks. But I meant what I said; they can't fix this.

After bringing them a pizza, they eventually know they can't linger and need to go leave, but they all give me hugs before they go. At least I know I'll still have friends at school until the end of the year when I graduate. They'll be Campbell's outside of school, and mine inside. That's fair.

What isn't fair is that my whole week is spent in the same work all day pattern, the occasional check in from Katie on my phone, but that's it, and I'm no closer to figuring out how to fix my relationship. The worst unfairness is that my mom is still in the hospital and I am getting zero information from my parents. I worry that in this case, no news is terrible news, but I have to keep working, to keep pretending everything is okay while I get people their orders.

On Friday after the game, all of my friends show up except Campbell. It's their Friday night tradition and at least we're slammed so I don't have to sit among them and pretend to be thrilled that they won.

Sunday afternoon we're crawling; we've had at most three full tables at one time since we opened, and I'm having a hard time keeping my eyes open. Working every waking hour of the day playing pretend and denying my feelings is wearing me down like over kneaded dough.

But Katie and Omar come in the door, and I'm more awake than I was just a minute ago. They're both unnaturally cautious as they walk up to me. Omar, his skin normally rich medium brown, looks like someone threw flour on him, splotchy white.

"What's going on?" I ask, not bothering with the clearly unnecessary regular greetings.

"Olivia, sit down with us, okay?" Katie asks, leading both Omar and I over to an alcove table.

"You're scaring me; he looks like crap," I say, nodding my head to Omar since my hands are twisted into my apron below the table.

"Campbell is moving back to the Dominican," Omar blurts out and I think I'm going to be sick.

"What?" I ask, my voice barely more than a whisper.

"He told me and Mom last night, that as soon as he can sell his car, he's going to buy a ticket and head back. I don't know what to do; he still won't talk to me about anything beyond pass the milk," he says, burying his face in his hands.

I'm not the only one whose heart is breaking because of this. Omar must wonder if he and Campbell will ever be close again if Campbell leaves before they can patch things up between them. Poor Carmen has no idea what's going on.

Campbell needed to go to school here, he said he couldn't afford the tuition for the high school in the Dominican; he also said he still had medical bills to pay off.

So, because of me, he's going back to the Dominican not accomplishing any of the goals that got him here.

"What have I done?" I ask, and a sob breaks loose from me.

"I'm sorry, I should never have tried. I've screwed this up for all of you." I run from the table, Katie and Omar calling after me. In the kitchen I pass Nelson, Junior, and Gina standing around talking.

"Junior," I say, hiccupping and unable to talk around my own closed throat.

"I got it," he says and heads to the dining room while I run up the stairs and to my bedroom.

CHAPTER 40

My bed is the perfect place to wallow in my own self pity, unable to see how I managed to utterly screw up so bad. I thought I was doing so well at life, at getting one. Ha. Not so much. My bed even has the added bonus of torturing me through color.

Part of me wonders if the lack of social life I've had means I am uniquely unable to handle the disaster I've made of the one I just got. But I decide that more likely is the explanation that I messed it all up so bad because of my lack of social skills.

The front door of our house opens after about an hour of nothing. I sit up in bed wondering why Junior would take the outside steps.

"Do you want to sit in the living room or the bedroom?" Dad asks, just outside my open door in the hallway.

I jump from my bed and dart to the hall where Dad is leading Mom as she shuffles her way along.

"Mom." My voice comes out in a wail as I fold her into my arms, the tears are instant and heavy. Holding her, she feels only marginally more substantial than she did in the hospital, but the house itself feels like it's more solidly held together because she's in it.

"Olivia, honey, don't cry. I'm okay," she says, and I pull back to kiss her cheek.

Dad and I lead her to the couch, dropping the blanket onto her lap and I run around getting her a cup of tea and a pillow to prop up her back.

"What are you doing home? Are you sure you're okay to be here?" I ask, after we've gotten her comfortable.

"Yes, I'm fine. We were only there a while to make sure everything was fine with my bones. And it is. Everything is fine, just the same issues as before, and we're dealing with that," she says, patting my hand and brushing my hair back from my face to tuck it behind my ear.

"Something about you seems sad. I told you, everything is okay," she says again and Junior thunders into the room to wrap her in a hug.

"I'm so glad you're home," he says.

The restaurant must be needing me to take his place again, so I stand to head back downstairs.

"Livvy, Dad's covering so I could say hi to Mom. You stay here as long as you need to," Junior says, getting up and squeezing my hand as he heads back to work.

"Why do you need to stay up here? Are you sick?" Mom asks, waving me toward her and putting the back of her hand to my forehead.

"No, just…" I don't want to burden her with my small problems. She doesn't need to feel bad that I failed so spectacularly at fulfilling her wish I get a life.

"Just, what, Livvy?"

I may as well throw out the burnt pizza now instead of staring at it any longer than I already have.

"Campbell broke up with me," I say, holding back the urge to lay in Mom's lap while she tells me everything will be okay.

"Oh, honey, I'm sorry," she says, as she sits up straighter, her mother's instinct turning her frailness to ferocity for a minute. "That is hard to handle, especially right now. Why would he do that? That's terrible."

"He, um, it's my fault. I'm not very good at social stuff still and I screwed it up." I sniff back the tears hovering at the edges of my lashes, swiping at my running nose.

"I find it hard to believe this is all your fault. And… wait…" She takes my hand and pulls me closer to her, staring into my eyes like she's mining my brain.

"You love him," she says, a soft smile on her face.

I nod, unable to trust my voice right now and she hugs me to her. I squeeze my eyes shut, willing the tears to go away. I should be nothing but thrilled that in this moment I have my mother home.

"Go get him, then," she says into my hair and I laugh into hers.

That night we close early and order in, the Mexican restaurant from down the street delivering to our door for our little celebration of Mom's return.

Dad is dishing up everyone's plates, splitting the many things we've ordered so we can each have some. Among the dishes are empanadas. I stare at one on my plate and am reminded of the time spent in Carmen's kitchen. The time spent with Campbell, learning his aunt's mastery of yucca. The time spent with him and our friends eating the Carmen fries and something lights up in my brain. If I was a cartoon a lightbulb wouldn't just go on above my head, it would be a million watt strobe flashing idea in Morse code.

"Hey, Junior, have you found an idea for the pizza competition tomorrow?" I ask, and three sets of eyes look at me, all confused by my random turn of the topic of conversation.

"Well, I've tried, but the one idea I had, it turns out Salvatore's is doing, a club sandwich pizza. His daughter dates one of my friends at school," he says.

"That's actually a pretty good idea, but the chicken, bacon, and white sauce on a pizza has been done before; it's barely new. Salvatore's is going to lose," I say.

"How do you know he's going to lose?" Dad asks.

"Because I have a better idea," I say, smiling wide for the first time in days.

"Please, I don't care how you do it, make him think Carmen wants you all to go, just get him there tomorrow. I know it's late notice, I'm sorry, but please," I beg Omar on the phone just ten minutes later while I shovel my food into my mouth, trying to get too much done in too short a period of time, and my family sits around me looking over my notebook with my paella pizza recipe in it.

"Okay, okay. I'll figure something out and we'll be there, but he might hate me for this," Omar says.

"He won't. I'm getting all the pieces together so he won't." I hang up the phone and before Junior can get a word out of his open mouth, I dial Katie.

"Olivia, what's up?" Katie asks.

"I have a plan to get Campbell back; can you be at the pizza competition tomorrow to hang out with Omar?" I ask.

"Hanging out with my boyfriend while I support my friend who is a pizza genius and it gets you and Campbell, my personal one true pairing back together, hmmm, let me think."

I can't help laughing.

"I'll text you the address and the time; you'll have to get out of school early," I say.

"Woo! Bonus," she says and laughs. "But I'm bringing Deacon."

"Perfect. Thanks, Katie."

We hang up and Junior, who has been staring at me, not so patiently waiting for his turn to talk immediately jumps in. "How did you think of this?"

"The paella was easy to think of as soon as I realized it wasn't about toppings, it's about creating the same flavor profiles as people's favorite foods. Theoretically you could do it with almost anything. But paella is extra cool because no one uses saffron and even fewer include seafood, so…" I gesture with my hands toward the notebook.

"Wow, Livvy. So you want the restaurant to use this recipe and use my entry for what, exactly?" Junior asks.

"I'm going to make an empanada pizza and call it *novio amoroso*," I say, smiling as I take another bite of my dinner.

"Livvy, that's so sweet," Mom says, and she smiles at me.

Dad looks decidedly less impressed with my idea; his face is screwed up in the you-are-not-right face.

"There are taco pizzas all over the place; we had one for a while, I don't see how that's new," he says.

"Well, good thing I'm not making a taco pizza then, huh? I'm making an empanada pizza with a yucca crust," I say.

"A yucca crust? How are you going to do that?" he asks, leaning forward and his face clears to being open.

"Campbell's aunt, Carmen, showed me how she works with yucca to get it to be more like a dough you can roll out. I'm going to use her instructions," I say. I down my last bite of dinner and stand up from my spot on the floor, picking my plate up off the coffee table and bringing it to the sink.

"So why are you in such a hurry?" Mom asks.

"Working the yucca means I need to get to the store to pick up what I need, and I have to experiment with it tonight so I'm ready for the competition by noon. You all just have to wake up early and follow my instructions." I rinse off my plate and put it in the dishwasher, as I head out of the room, I see from the corner of my eye that Junior is heading to my notebook with a pen.

"No, Junior." I stop and point a finger in his direction. "Whatever change you think would work better on that recipe, it won't. I've tested every possible idea you could think up. My recipe is right; don't screw with it."

"But, what if the saffron is just in the dough; this seems like overkill," he says, reaching toward the notebook.

I look at Dad, one eyebrow up, and he reaches out a hand to stop Junior from making a single mark in my notebook.

"Testing is always better at working through the kinks, Junior. Your sister is right. We'll follow her recipe," he says and Junior slumps back.

"Love you all. See you tomorrow," I say, waving as I grab my phone, my wallet, and my keys.

The walk to the grocery store is long and cold with winter coming in fast, but it helps to clear the last vestiges of doubt from my mind. This is going to work. I will get Campbell back. I will prove to him that he is exactly what I want.

He thinks my plans are more important to me than he is, but he's wrong. My plans don't mean much if I'm left without him and my friends. Mom was right when she said I needed to find a better balance, to have more than the restaurant to care about. Now what I care about most are the people in my life, and one person in particular.

In my mind I start to picture a different restaurant, one that allows all of my family to have more room for life outside our grand dame house, either level of it. I picture a restaurant with the kind of atmosphere I want, with the food I want, with more smells than just pizza, and with Campbell by my side while I make it happen.

My phone is in my pocket, but it's starting to feel heavy and I know I can't wait to start making changes. I pull it out and text to Mom and Dad and Junior in a family chat. Laying out the things I know we need right now and the things we need to implement over time. I also lay out my vision for the restaurant for the future.

The phone is silent for the rest of my walk and that's okay. Whether they like my suggestions or not, it doesn't matter. Because I will have that restaurant one day, the one in my mind. I will make it happen, even if it isn't Joe's. Now all I have to do is make sure the right person is with me for the ride.

Going through the grocery store is a mundane task and I've heard a lot of people complain about it over the years, but I love it. I love finding the fresh produce, smelling the bakery, and I enjoy seeing any new products.

I may not love the front of the house part of the restaurant business, and I don't think that will ever change, but I adore the back of the house. The food is love and community, culture and family. If the kitchen is the heart of the home, the food is the life's blood.

By the time I make the walk back to the restaurant, my fingers are frozen where they're wrapped around my bags, but I'm not bothered. I'm too thrilled to be creating this love letter in pizza.

In the parking lot of the restaurant, I'm surprised to see Deacon and Katie, stomping their feet and blowing on their hands.

"What are you doing here?" I ask, running to get to them and get them inside before they freeze.

"You said you were working in here tonight. I've been calling you," she says.

"No, I have my phone in my pocket," I fumble with my bags, handing them off to Deacon so I can dig out my keys and phone.

I check the phone as I open the door and it's dead.

"Oh, oops. Sorry guys," I say, holding it up for them to see. "Here, let me take those." I reach for the bags and set them all out on the counter while I plug my phone in to the dock in the office and turn all the lights on as I go through the restaurant.

"So, why are you here again?" I ask, unpacking the bags and moving through the kitchen to collect all the things I need.

"You're our alibi. We had to come up with a good reason for not going to school tomorrow, so I made up a story about you needing us, life and death, blah blah. Anyway, here we are, your assistants," Katie says, holding her hands out in a ta-da motion.

I take them in, these incredible friends of mine and I don't try to hold back the tears that fall down my cheeks, or the smile that's so big my face hurts.

"Thank you," I say, it isn't enough to explain to them how much it means they're doing this for me, but it's all I have at the moment.

"Oh, Olivia," Katie says, grabbing me and pulling me into a hug.

Deacon grabs us both, wrapping us up and lifting us in the air as we laugh.

"Let's get to work," I say.

CHAPTER 42

We work through the night, preparing the yucca, more than enough for multiple crusts, because I'm not sure of exactly how this recipe would be best to prepare. At three in the morning, the first of our pizzas with different combinations of sauce, toppings, and cheeses come out of the oven. The only one not exhausted is Deacon, who looks like he could do this forever.

"You are way too chipper for this early in the morning after no sleep," I say, pulling the last of the pies out of the oven.

"Are you kidding? This is the best part. We finally get to eat," he says, with a fist in the air.

Katie and I laugh, but she says, "I hope one of these works, because I need to sleep if I'm going to be awake enough to get you all ready for tomorrow." She yawns so large her jaw pops.

"Stop that," I say, yawning in chorus with her. "What do you mean, all ready for tomorrow, I just need the pizza to be ready and I'm fine."

"That's cute," she says, her head cocked to the side.

I dart a look at Deacon, who shrugs; he doesn't have a clue what she's talking about either.

"Oh, come on. You two are ridiculous," she says, throwing her hands up in the air. "The pure one and the only thinks about food one. You both need me in your lives, that's all I'm saying."

"Yes, we're very grateful," Deacon says, while I cut the pizzas for us to sample and try not to laugh. "Get to the point."

"This is all to get Campbell back to Olivia, not to a pizza. We need to make Olivia as appetizing as the food." She raises an eyebrow and Deacon and I both open our mouths.

I swear he's thinking what I am, oh. Duh. Okay.

"Well, I can't exactly wear an oversized white t-shirt and white socks with nothing else to this thing," I mumble as I plate up our pizzas.

"You," she's laughing, tears are leaking out of the corners of her eyes she's laughing so hard and I realize I said it out loud. "Wow, okay then."

"Stop. You weren't supposed to hear that," I say, my face an inferno.

"No, that's hot. I'm with my dude on this," Deacon says, nodding and grabbing his plate, eyes wide.

"Let's just pretend that didn't happen. Here, Katie," I say, trying to not look as she wipes the tears away and bites her lips to keep from laughing more.

"Ready, one, two, three," I say, and we all take a bite.

Deacon screws up his face as he chews, Katie tries to hide the fact she's spitting it back onto her plate, and I know the minute it's in my mouth that I've failed. The yucca isn't done all the way.

"Oh, god. This is gross," I say, spitting mine back onto the plate.

"Maybe one of the others will be good," Deacon says, picking up a different piece.

"No, the crust isn't done," I put my plate aside and drop my face into my hands.

"So, do we need to put it back in the oven for a while?" Katie asks, inspecting the pieces on her plate like looking at them from a different angle will give her the answer.

"Then all the toppings will burn. I failed," I say. My voice is flat, all the air has gone out of me and the images I had on my walk start to float away.

"How is it so different when it's in an actual empanada?" Deacon asks, his voice is wistful and he's staring at his plate like he's mourning the food on it.

"Empanadas are fried," I say, rubbing my hands into my eyes, trying to wake myself up for another try, trying not to give in to how tired I am.

"Can we fry a pizza?" Katie asks, as she yawns again so her words sound like caw we fraw a pizza.

"What on earth did you just say?" Deacon asks.

"You don't speak yawn?" I ask, laughing, but then I stop. "She asked if we can fry a pizza." I get up and start dumping my plate and the destroyed pizzas into the trash, my fatigue long gone.

"Which you can't, that would ruin a pizza," Deacon says, shaking his head as he grabs Katie's plate and his to solemnly dump them too.

"No, but I can fry the dough before I put it in the oven," I say, rushing to start again.

"That's brilliant," Deacon says, helping me. "Where's Katie?"

I look back to the table and she's stretched out on the bench in the alcove, fast asleep.

"We should let her sleep," Deacon says, a soft smile on his face.

"You too are so close for cousins; I barely know mine. They live all the way across the country," I say, rolling out more yucca for a fresh dough.

"Our birthdays are super close, we were raised almost like twins, but our whole extended family is super close," he says with a smile.

I envy them, I wish we had closer relationships with our extended family. But looking at Deacon I realize that without trying, in my little attempt to just make a friend or two, I gained a version of extended family for myself.

We work side by side and have to fry the dough one part at a time as the whole thing doesn't fit in the wok, the biggest pan I can find. I grab my apron and twist it as it fries, paying extra attention to the areas I worry will get overcooked.

Deacon reaches out and unwraps my hand from my apron.

"It will work," he says.

I nod, and we get back to work.

When we add the toppings, we divvy up the pie into sections for each of the possible combinations, making the most out of the crust we've made.

Pulling it out of the oven, the smell is right at least, giving off all of the aromas of Carmen's kitchen when she made us the empanadas.

"Smells great," Deacon says, wiping his mouth and making me wonder if he's actually drooling.

We have been working for hours and haven't eaten anything, so I can't hold it against him. I plate six different pieces for him, his larger slices than mine, and we sit down to eat.

The first bite isn't quite right so I set that piece aside.

"It's not bad," Deacon says, continuing to eat the rest of the piece. "It's not the one for the competition, but it's edible and the crust works this time.

The next one is better. But I still set it aside.

"Mmm, this one is better," Deacon says, following with me, mowing his down like it's his job.

The one after that is really wrong, it goes in the hard no pile.

"Nope, don't like this one," Deacon says, although he finishes the slice.

The fourth piece… Oh, the fourth piece.

"Holy empanadas, Batman, this one is amazing," Deacon says, and he slows down his chewing, closing his eyes on the bite in his mouth.

"It's perfect," I say, closing my eyes too, and letting all my hopes for the future flood back to me.

CHAPTER 43

Before I start on making my last pizza for the competition, I decide I have time to sleep a little while. It's almost five in the morning. I need to be up and getting things going by eight at the latest.

Deacon helps me clean up and we put my yucca dough away in the walk in along with all of my toppings, clearly labeled as do not touch.

I grab my now charged phone from the office and set an alarm for seven thirty, then he picks Katie up in a fireman's carry and we head upstairs to my house.

He puts her in my bed, and I get him comfortable on the couch before I join her in the bed; the minute my head is no longer vertical I'm asleep. But I take my imagined future with me, the one in which I have it all.

The alarm goes off in the middle of a dream in which I'm kissing Campbell. I've never in my life wanted to throw my phone in the garbage disposal more than I do right now.

I roll over and groan into the pillow that now only vaguely now smells like peaches.

"What in the hell is that noise and who do I have to beg to make it go away forever?" Katie asks as I reach over and turn the damn thing off.

"You can sleep a while longer," I say, throwing my legs over the side of the bed and rubbing my hands over my face, "I need to cook."

"Nope. You're not getting away from me that easy," she says, getting out of the bed and dragging her fingers through her hair.

"I'm going to hop in the shower and then get to work cooking; can you do whatever you're planning while I get things done?" I ask, grabbing a towel out of my drawer and heading into the bathroom.

"Of course, and I'm going to rifle through your clothes while you shower," she says on the other side of my door.

I shake my head and get to brushing my teeth and showering while she hunts for clothes designed to get Campbell to look at me. Personally, I don't think it has anything to do with clothes, but she is infinitely smarter in this area than I am, and it can't hurt. My shower doesn't last too long; I can't let it. I have things to do.

When I walk out of the bathroom, Katie is sitting on my bed, wearing some of my clothes that I would never think to put together and looking amazing as she puts on makeup from her giant purse.

"Am I supposed to cook in a towel?" I ask.

"Right here," she says, gesturing to a pile of shorts and a button up shirt.

"That is not at all what I thought you would suggest," I say, grabbing a bra and panties out of my drawer.

"Well, that's because I wouldn't let you out of the house in this. This is just for while you cook. I'm still thinking about what you're going to wear for the competition."

"Okay," I say, shaking my head at how serious she is while I get dressed in my temporary clothes and run a brush through my hair really quick, sure I haven't even gotten all the tangles out of it.

In the kitchen, I start by getting the sauce going, making sure to make enough.

Next, I prepare four small pizza crusts while the oil gets to the proper temperature. I'm going to make four personal pan sized pizzas so I can fit the entire crust in the pan to fry all at once, I'm taking no chances that there will be an uneven fry.

The last step is to put it all together, and I'm doing that when Deacon sits up on the couch, groaning.

"You are the noisiest cook in history," he says, rubbing his eyes.

"Sorry, Deacon. I don't have time to be slow today. I need to get these done, and still have twenty minutes to get ready," I say, closing one of the oven doors on the first two pizzas and moving on to put the last two in the other oven.

"What do you need me to do?" he asks, getting up and grabbing a peppermint candy from a tray of them on the counter.

"Can you run downstairs and get me four personal pan boxes?" I ask as Katie comes out of my room and gestures me into a chair at the table.

"Sit, my turn," she says.

Deacon disappears down the stairs while Katie yanks my hair through a brush and works whatever magic it is that she possesses on my hair. She moves onto my makeup while Deacon comes back with the boxes.

"Your brother and your dad are down their cooking your paella pizza; did you know that?" he asks, setting the boxes on the counter.

"She knows," my mom says from behind me. "It was her idea."

"Mom, this is Katie and Deacon, my friends. Guys, this is my mother, Angela," I say, and they all say their hellos while the timer for the pizzas goes off.

I scramble from the table into the kitchen and check the pizzas, perfect, before I take them out and put them in the boxes.

"Alright, we've got to hurry up," I say, and Katie grabs me by the hand to drag me into my room.

She finishes my makeup and starts unbuttoning my shirt. I open my eyes to help her.

"Nope. Shut them. I want you to be surprised today too," she says.

I look at her hard, but I'm smiling and follow her instructions as she gets me undone and put back together again. By the time she's done I'm bouncing. There's too much riding on today for me to contain it all inside my body and I'm trying really hard not to have shaking hands. Instead, I'm left bouncing while Katie repeatedly puts a hand on my shoulder and holds me down until I stop.

"Now follow me," she says, pulling me out into the hall.

"Livvy, you look beautiful," Mom says.

"Yep, good choice," Deacon says.

"Seriously, Katie. I need to see this," I say, bouncing again.

"Open your eyes," Katie says.

When I do and look down at myself, I suck in a breath. The last thing I expected was for her to pick out my dress from her party.

"But… what if this is a bad idea?" I ask, all my bouncing is over.

"Trust me, it isn't a bad idea. He was in awe of you that night. This is perfect," Katie says.

"I don't have time to change anyway. And I need a coat," I say running back into my room to grab my shoes.

When I come back into the living room Mom has a long red sweater for me to put on over my dress. It's beautiful in its own right and I'm happy I get to bring some of Mom with me.

"Thanks," I say and get my shoes on while Deacon and Katie each grab a box of pizza and I grab two.

I kiss my mom on the cheek, she waves goodbye from the couch and we file out the door and down the steps.

"Olivia, slow down," Katie says when I hit the parking lot almost running.

She's right. If I don't slow down, I'm likely to trip and that would be a disaster.

We pile into Deacon's car and he gets us to the venue, navigating the downtown traffic with the ease of someone long on practice in the area, who knows all the streets he can turn down to avoid Mercer or the other roads that are constantly clogged.

Pulling into the parking lot, the building looms before me and no matter how much effort I put into my hands not shaking, they do.

"Guys," I say, my voice hushed.

Deacon and Katie turn in their seats to look at me in the back.

"Is this going to work?" I ask, and they glance at each other. "You don't think it will, do you? You think I'm a fool, and I'm doing it all for nothing." I close my eyes and slump back into the seat taking deep breaths, trying not to hyperventilate.

"Olivia, this is going to work," Deacon says. "No one would be able to resist the kind of grand romantic gesture you're doing here."

"I don't know what made him break up with you in the first place," Katie says, "but I have a hard time imagining a world in which you two don't get back together eventually. You're too good together."

Opening my eyes to look at them and the building looming

behind them, I'm not as sure. And I don't believe they are either. But I've come too far to turn back now. This is my chance, I'm taking it.

"Let's go," I say, opening my door.

The inside of the auditorium feels like being at the state fair, the crowds, moving in any direction they please, the booths around the edge of the room where each person has a small placard with their name or their restaurant's name and a warming dish on which to display their pizza.

We pass a myriad of terrible looking options, like a desert pizza with too many different flavored drizzled toppings. But the worst one we pass must be a tuna fish sandwich pizza. We don't stick around to read the name of it on their sign because the smell is awful. I feel bad for the people in the booths to either side of them.

Skirting through the throng, we're careful to avoid a collision with any of our boxes of our pizzas.

The booth with the Joe's name on it is right next to the booth with our last name on it. Although the Joe's booth is technically mine, the one I belong in for today isn't the one for the restaurant. My dad and brother aren't here yet with theirs, but they will be.

My booth has options on the shelves beneath the tabletop of

what size warming tray I want. I pick the three personal pan sized ones.

"Does that mean I get to eat the last one?" Deacon asks, and it's his turn to bounce.

"That's for Campbell," Katie says and smacks him on the arm.

"Sorry," I say, although I'm only half listening to them as I set up the sign that reads the name of my pizza and make sure each one is cut perfectly and turned exactly right.

A bell rings and my knees join my hands in shaking.

"Where are my dad and Junior?" I ask, not really looking for an answer, but thinking out loud.

"They'll be here, I'm sure of it," Katie says, putting her hands on mine and giving them a squeeze.

Her phone chimes in her pocket and she pulls it out to check it.

"Omar is here with Campbell and Carmen," she says, and pulls me into a hug. "We've got to go. Good luck, you're going to be great."

Deacon gives me a hug too before following after her to be swallowed up by the crowd. My hands are shaking so bad the tremors are moving up my arms. I ball them into fists to try and force them to stop, my short fingernails digging into my palms.

Dad and Junior come through the crowd, all at once. They aren't anywhere that I can see one minute and the next they're beside me setting up their booth. I get to work helping them, the three of us moving in concert without a word being spoken. Junior is entering the pizza's name in their sign and I'm getting the warming tray from underneath the booth and plugging it in.

Their pizza looks amazing and when I look up at the sign, it reads: Livvy's Favorite Flavor Paella Pizza.

"Dad," I say, and I can't get anything else out, my hands are wrapped around each other, pressing against my lips so the pressure will relieve the one building in my eyes that means I might cry.

"It was Junior's idea," he says, and puts an arm around me.

My brother smiles at me and pats me on the shoulder.

"You deserve it, Livvy," he says.

The bell chimes again and the crowd disperses to the sides of the room, we all take our places at our booths, and wait.

Judges for food contests come in two varieties, the kind that linger over each entry, examining it from every angle, and the kind that speed through, taking a nibble and a glance that misses nothing. In both cases, the best competitions have someone following behind the judge to hand them a new card for each entry and that person keeps track of the mounting, and often burdensome paperwork. These judges are the type that know and decide in a second.

I have always been fascinated by the people who pass judgement on food. I want to know what they do in their spare time. When your palate is that refined does food lose all the beauty? If I go to an event, I want to sit back and enjoy the overcooked chicken made by someone's mom that she's weirdly proud of, I don't want to dissect it, but these people do.

Those in the crowd not connected to a booth, of which there are fewer than I expect, follow in the judges wake, watching and smelling the aromas. Just like those of us with entries, they must be trying to figure out which pizzas the judges like.

Deacon is so close to the judges and their paperwork helpers it's like he's a part of the group. Because of the sheer size of him, I'm surprised as the group nears Dad and Junior's booth that they aren't frightened by him looming behind them. His want of their job might get him in trouble.

I cross my fingers for him and ball my hands back into fists, holding them behind my back so they don't see. My knees are pressing against each other and I hold my breath while they're at my booth, trying my food.

One judge's eyes pop open wide when they take a bite and I have no idea how to interpret that look.

After the judges are past me, I scan the crowd trailing them. Katie said Campbell is here, but the people pass me, and I don't see him.

My hands loosen from their fists behind me and drop to my sides; he must have left.

But when the crowd parts in front of me, he's there, standing next to Carmen and Omar who has his arm around Katie.

Campbell is staring right at me.

My breathing hitches in my chest, my heart is ringing louder and faster than any bell they used to get us into our places.

His eyes raise to read the name of my entry and the name of the entry next to me, my Dad and Junior's. He looks back at me and smiles.

CHAPTER 45

Campbell walks up to me, across the ugly carpet of the room, and it doesn't matter that the lighting in here isn't the best, the fluorescent tubes casting everything faintly yellower than it should be, he is beautiful.

He's just wearing jeans and a sweater, I am over dressed for this moment, but I don't care. My dress feels too tight for me to catch my breath, but I hope it does its job.

Please do the job, dress. Please.

"Beloved boyfriend," he says when he gets to me, translating the name of my pizza on my sign.

"I had one who inspired the recipe," I say, and his brows draw together. He looks beyond me to the pizza on my table, the pizza clearly not the one we worked on together. "It's empanada."

Half his mouth quirks up in that smile of his and sparks dance at the edges of my vision.

"Olivia, *que linda*," he says, and he takes a step closer to me. "I have some apologizing to do. I..." he trails off and clears his throat, his eyes darting to where my dad and brother are clearly listening to our conversation.

"When I got to my house that day, I saw Omar kiss you and I thought..." he says, and shakes his head.

"That's why?" I ask. "Because of our stupid plan? Campbell, no. He kissed me on the cheek and hugged me because I said I loved you."

"Wait, you said you loved me?" he asks, stepping closer to me still and I think he must hear my heart, its beating is drowning out all the background noise so all I can hear is him.

"I still do," I say, the first time I've ever told anyone outside my family that I love them.

He takes my hand then and a tear falls, making a track down his cheek, hanging on to the edge of his jaw.

"I love you," he says.

My dad and my brother are standing right next to us, his aunt, his cousin, and our friend are behind him, but I don't care. I fold myself into his arms and pull his face to mine, kissing him in a way that I hope makes up for all the days I didn't get to.

When he pulls back from me, I reach a hand, blessedly devoid of shaking, up to wipe away his tears. The sound around us filters back in and I realize Omar is whistling and the others are clapping.

"You guys are the weirdest family members," I say and duck my head into Campbell's chest while my cheeks flame and he laughs.

I reach under the table to hand him his own box of the pizza I made for him, he takes one bite and closes his eyes, his mouth turning up into a smile as he chews.

"Tia, you have to try this."

My dad and Junior are introduced all around and everyone tries the different pizza we created, eating the last of the slices.

Campbell and I walk hand in hand at the back of the group to the stage where the announcement of the winner will be.

"I think you're going to win," Deacon says, finding us and joining the group.

"Thanks, but I already did, and you aren't a judge yet," I say, and he grins.

Deacon reaches out a giant fist, shoves Campbell's shoulder with it and fist bumps me before he turns around to face the stage.

"You should win. You deserve the restaurant. It would be in good hands with you," Campbell says, raising my hand to kiss the back of it.

"Even if I don't, I've decided I will start my own somehow. I want to serve Carmen fries and deserts, but only the baked kind of deserts, like cinnamon rolls," I say, leaning into his side. In my head all the images I had of us running a restaurant together start to play again. This time there is no pain or doubt tagging along with them. This time all I have is hope.

"Now that's the kind of restaurant I would want to eat every meal at," he says and kisses my forehead.

The bell chimes again and the conversations going on around us wither and die out.

"Pizza lovers, welcome to Seattle's Best New Pizza," the stern looking woman at the microphone says. "Thank you for all the imaginative and tasty recipes. I can safely speak for all of my fellow judges when I say the quality of the entries was inspiring."

She drones on about the sponsors and the prizes.

"I've got the best prize," I whisper to Campbell who leans down and kisses me until Dad coughs in front of us.

We pull apart and I bite my lip looking up at my father.

"Livvy, the restaurant is going to be yours; you more than proved yourself. I'm sorry I ever doubted this was for you.

Good job, baby," Dad says, his voice hushed so we don't interrupt the lady's speech and he turns around to face the stage again.

I look at Campbell, my mouth hanging open. This is it. The reason I entered the contest in the first place, and I have it.

"Now you really won," he says and hugs me tight.

"So, without further ado, the second runner up for the best pizza goes to Salvatore's for their club sandwich pizza."

The crowd cheers and Junior looks at me with his eyebrows raised.

Yeah, yeah, he was right. I never said it was bad, just not original.

"Well done. The first runner up is by a Carrasio."

At the sound of my last name, I grab onto my dad's sleeve in front of me with one hand and squeeze Campbell's hand with my other until I'm sure I'm hurting him.

"The empanada pizza, *Novio Amoroso*."

People are cheering, none louder than my little corner of supporters. I won second place with a pizza I made up last night. My laugh is louder than Omar's whistle or Campbell yelling. It's even louder than Deacon's deep, booming whoops. My dad turns around and picks me up in a hug.

"Very well done."

We all stifle our celebration so she can go on, but there's no suppressing the smiles on all of our faces, none of us expected this, not really, no matter how much they told me they did so I would keep going.

"And the winner, and the one who can officially say they serve Seattle's Best Pizza is..." She waits far longer than is necessary, most the people in the crowd staring at her and hanging on her every syllable.

Of course, all of us are still silently giving high fives and pumping our fists at each other, our quiet thrill of a good place finish waiting less than patiently until we can scream about my accomplishment again. We don't care who wins at this point.

"Joe's for Livvy's Favorite Flavor Paella Pizza."

"What?" I scream and I don't even know who hugs me first, or who is loudest this time. People in the crowd congratulate my dad, shake his hand, and he keeps telling them it was my recipe, but none of them can get to me for congratulations. My friends, my brother, and my boyfriend are an impenetrable wall of joy around me.

CHAPTER 46

It's been six months since I won; the sign over the door now reads Joe's, home of Seattle's Best Pizza, Livvy's Favorite Flavor. I still have a month until I graduate, but Dad is already taking a step back from the business and letting me make some decisions. Like promoting Nelson to back of the house manager, and Campbell and Gina to front of the house managers. I also get to make every single decision about the menu.

Tonight, we're closed for a private party.

"Shhh," Campbell says as Deacon bumps into a table in the dark.

"Sorry," he says, too loud and gets shushed again.

"Way too pure," I whisper. Campbell shushes me with a kiss, and we pull apart when we hear the clicking of the door opening.

"This is silly, Joe. Can you take this thing off my eyes now, please?" Mom's voice floats through the darkened, silent restaurant, and Junior, home for a visit from med school, crouched down next to me, buries his face in his arm so no one hears his laugh.

I still do, so I nudge him with my elbow.

The lights flick on.

"Where is everyone?" Mom's voice asks.

"Surprise!" The whole room full of friends and family jumps up and my mother puts a hand to her mouth to cover the giant smile.

Her head is still wrapped in a scarf, but there's fuzz growing back. She's done with her chemo, and today, Dad called to say they got the news from the doctors she's cancer free.

For an impromptu party, we managed to get close to one hundred people to drop everything and celebrate my mother, who has tears pouring down her cheeks as she laughs.

I wait my turn, Campbell's arm around me, as she makes her way through the room accepting congratulations from everyone.

When it's my turn, I'm crying as much as she is and we fold into a hug, neither of us going to the other, but meeting in the middle.

"You did this, didn't you?" she asks into my hair.

"I don't know what you're talking about," I say and kiss her damp cheek before I step back to wipe my tears away.

"Of course she did," Campbell says, hugging Mom too. "Olivia never does anything half way."

Mom moves on to Junior and continues to make her way around the room. Omar and Katie aren't together anymore, but they're both here and I watch them greet her with warmth. Theresa introduces Mom to Rebecca, her girlfriend. And Deacon lifts my still underweight mother into the air in a twirling hug while she squeals.

These friends of mine have become family, each of them

with some piece of the menu inspired by them, whether they know it or not.

"What are you thinking, *linda*?" Campbell says, taking me by the hand and pulling me onto his lap at one of the tables.

My mind wasn't on anything in particular, but I look at his long graceful fingers and something occurs to me, a way to give Campbell back a little something that he thinks he lost.

"Do you still love to play pool?" I ask and his eyes get big.

"Um, not at all what I thought you were going to say, but yes. When no one is around to complain about how good I am, I play at home," he says, lacing his fingers with mine.

"Have you thought about teaching other people how you do your magic?" I ask and am rewarded with his mouth dropping open and then his half smile appearing.

"You really are going to kill me," he says, putting his forehead to mine.

"That wouldn't kill you." I kiss the end of his nose because I can't get to his lips.

"No. But being this happy might." He raises his head and kisses me while our little corner of the universe celebrates around us and the smells I personally love, of peaches, pizza, and enchiladas make everything better and tell me I'm home.

THANK YOU FOR READING!

If you enjoyed this book please leave a review at your favorite vendor.

If you would like to be the first to know about the next book in the series and get a free ebook head on over to darleneeverly.com and sign up for the newsletter.

ACKNOWLEDGMENTS

A whole hearted thank you to Bean, the Rottens, and all of my friends and family. A big bag of thanks to Jupiter Alley and Magnolia editing for their help in making this happen, as well as the team at Wishing Well. Sometimes, when you least expect it, characters don't break your heart.